For my mom,

who taught me that women are

superheroes.

ARCHENEMY PRESS

First Edition – October, 2016

Paperback ISBN-10 0-9977198-0-X

Paperback ISBN-13 978-0-9977198-0-2

Digital ISBN-10 0-9977198-1-8

Digital ISBN-13 978-0-9977198-1-9

Hardcover ISBN-10 0-9977198-2-6

Hardcover ISBN-13 978-0-9977198-2-6

James T. Egan – Cover Art

Contents

Contents

Hannah The Huntress

Book 1: Blood Legacy

By Saul Bishop

I write to

give myself

strength.

I write to be

The characters

that I am not.

I write to

explore all

the things

I'm afraid of.

- Joss Whedon

This is how you do it:

you sit down at the

keyboard and you put

one word after another

until it's done.

It's that easy,

and that hard.

-Neil Gaiman

Prologue: The Cowboy and the Elephant

The mad Buddha laughed, a howl that echoed across the dark landscape and disappeared into the far away hills. Down the talus and the tor flowed a lazy shallow stream, winding and curving through the eastern prairie before emptying into a pond beside a bodhi tree. It was beneath the leaves where the man sat, a westerner traveling the world, studying the supernatural, seeking the divine. He was tall, grim, and of singular purpose, a searcher sitting under a fig tree in India wearing cowboy boots, jeans, and a checkered shirt. He was out of place, and he knew it, what's more, even the local gods he sought knew it. His night of silent contemplation ended when out of the ether he heard a voice, and upon opening his eyes saw an elephant standing there, talking, in what sounded like a British accent.

"What is your name?" Asked the elephant.

"Kord." Said the cowboy.

"Ask your questions," said Ganesh, "and make them somewhat interesting."

The man, now with tears running down his cheeks said, "Please, tell me what's going to happen."

For a moment the old elephant stood there, a long awkward moment, then he walked over to the pond, lowered his trunk and began to drink. The water moved as a small whirlpool formed in the center while the elephant filled himself, images of marvelous events and the faces of strangers rose to the surface, and were gone again as quick as they had appeared, in his head the cowboy mage heard the voices of those he had never met. Turning around to face the man, the elephant lifted his head high and blew the water into the sky; this astonished the man but soon he understood, in each drop he saw the future, a multiverse of possibilities fell around him.

As he sat, he lifted his face to feel the water, and raised his arms in welcome to the magic within them. "Am I hallucinating?" Asked the cowboy zen wizard.

"Of course you are," replied the talking elephant. "How else do you expect to see the futures?"

The man saw hope and horror, he saw all of the hate in the world and the love that eclipsed it, and after searching for so long he was finally calm inside. The sensation though was fleeting, abruptly he twisted his body, oddly and with serpentine grace, and when he stopped he looked out onto Serenity and began to laugh. A slow guffaw that built until a minute later when the man beneath the tree was howling, enlightened with madness and the realization that what will be cannot be altered or overcome. A thousand paths with only one destination at the terminus.

Old Ganesh looked down at the man and said, "Now is the Kali Yuga, little mage, there was nowhere else your questions could have led."

"You have to tell her," said the cowboy through fits of laughter. "You have to warn her that they're coming, that they're all coming back."

"No, little mage," said Ganesh. "That is your burden and yours alone, all that I can do is show you the way, it is your choice as to whether you walk it or not."

The cowboy shook and gasped as he continued to laugh, fell over onto his side and threw up as a water snake slithered from his mouth and made its way to the pond, disappearing beneath the surface. For a while he was silent, his thoughts far away, but soon he started to shriek again, his body convulsing from the effort. Ganesh looked down upon him with sympathy, his compassion radiant; and as he left, the silence of his stride was eerie and impossible, the sound of endless laughter his companion.

Chapter 1: School Night

It was a little before midnight when the would be robber approached the young family of three walking down the alley. They had been to a movie, an end of summer stay-up-too-late treat for their eight year old son the night before school started. A chill in the air had convinced them to take a shortcut through the alley to their car, as they walked through discussing the movie an orange tomcat hissed at them from on top of a dumpster, its fur was raised and its eyes glowed green in the dark but as quick as it had appeared it vanished from sight. The little boy was reenacting the sound effects and the action scenes to his parents when they were confronted by an assailant; the man had a small pistol in his right hand pointed at them and he was softly singing Frank Sinatra's *I've Got You Under My Skin*.

"Give me everything you've got," he said. "Hurry up, hurry up, hurry up." His gnarled and twisted hands were shaking and his pupils were too large; sweat dripped from his forehead into his eyes and unkempt hair,
he gnashed his teeth together so loud that everyone could hear. The family was terrified, the mom and dad attempted to hide the little boy behind them but this only provoked the irrational behavior of the robber more. "What you tryin' to do? Don't you do that. Gimme your money. Now!" He slew his words and careened from side to side like a boat on the

water, but his gun remained pointing straight ahead, never wavering.

The father threw his wallet and his wife's purse to the ground. "Here, take whatever we have, but please, leave us alone." Somehow this made the robber angrier and more incoherent, he started to swear and mumble and threaten incoherently. He looked towards the boy and leveled the gun at where he was hiding behind his mother. The parents began to weep, to beg, the boy sobbed into his mom's pant leg, unable to look up; and with a wicked smile through rotted teeth the robber stopped shaking, took a step forward, leveled his gun closer and said, "Time to die."

Watching the events play out was a young girl in her late teens crouched above on a fire escape. She had long black hair, green eyes, and wore a Public Enemy t-shirt beneath a black jacket; her jeans were designer and her Chuck Taylor's were so shiny and red that they practically gave her away. A relentless stream of thoughts and anxieties went through her head as she looked below. *What should I do? What if I get them killed? What if I get killed?* But those thoughts only lasted a moment, maybe a breath and no more. She climbed onto the highest rail of the fire escape and somersaulted down on top of the robber. Her foot hit his outstretched arm, knocking the gun out of his hand, as she landed she came to a halt in front of him, kneeling to gather her balance she sprang up and punched him in the jaw sending him two feet in the air and into a pile of garbage. He landed with a dull thud. Getting up, the bad man, dazed, swung at her and missed, she hit him with a right cross, and watched as he toppled over, unconscious.

Standing to the side beside a dumpster the family huddled together holding each other tight, the shock and disbelief of what had just happened clearly displayed on their faces. After a moment the little boy untangled himself from his folks' embrace and walked over to the girl, hugging her as hard as he could. "Thank you," he said.

"You're very welcome," said the girl. She smiled and with her coat sleeve dried the tears from the little boy's cheeks.

"Who are you?" He said with a voice full of awe.

"I'm Hannah," she said.

"Wh-what are you?" He stammered.

Hannah thought about that for a second and then leaned over to whisper in his ear, "I'm a superhero."

"Whoa. That is so cool," he said.

"It's a bit of a secret though, so don't go telling a lot of people. Okay?" Said Hannah.

"Okay, I promise." He said.

"Now what's your name, mister?" She said.

"Tommy," he said. And as she was about to say something else he yelled over to his parents, who really, were standing right next to him. "Mom, dad, Hannah saved us." Before she could back away the girl found herself being hugged by the whole family, a dozen thank yous spilled out followed by a dozen more and at last they let her go. Emotionally drained and not knowing what else to do everyone grew quiet and began staring at their feet.

"Well, Tommy, why don't you guys get home, I'll use my spider webbing to tie this loser up and then I'll leave a note for the police to pick him up." They all looked at her in complete confusion, even the kid. "Um, spider webs… it's how Spider-Man trusses up his bad guys."

It took a few seconds but they got it. "Oh," they all kind of said at once.

The mom picked up little Tommy and walked to the end of the alley, he stared over her shoulder at Hannah the entire time, smiling and waving as they disappeared around the corner. The dad held back a minute and digging into his recovered wallet he pulled out a business card and handed it to Hannah. It said August Winslow M.D. on it along with a couple of phone numbers and an office address. "I owe you everything," he said. "If you ever need help call that number and I'll be there."

"Thanks," said Hannah. "If I make a hobby of this knowing a doctor might be pretty useful."

"Be careful," he said. Turning around he walked off towards his family down the alley until he too was gone.

For a while Hannah stood there not moving, she listened to her beating heart as it took its time slowing down from the adrenaline. The world seemed calm after what had just happened. For a few minutes anyway.

Out of the silence a voice echoed down the alley from the far entrance where the family had gone. "Really? You went with a Spider-Man reference there? Because I could swear that was a moment for a Batman pop culture nod if ever there was one."

Hannah was surprised by the stranger's sudden appearance. She tensed up, readying herself in case something was about to happen. As he walked towards her she thought he must be older, he had snowy white hair and he was wearing a black suit with a white shirt along with a purple vest and tie. He was using a dark cherry wood cane with his right hand and he had a flashlight in his left, once he was closer though she realized that he wasn't carrying anything but instead had a small orb full of bright light that floated above his slightly outstretched hand. His face however was the surprise, despite his clothing and unnaturally ashen hair he was young; her age, maybe a year or two older. *The face of a damaged angel,* she thought, for over his left eye a long faded scar ran from above his brow to the middle of his cheek, and his smile held mischief.

Hannah looked at him with cool eyes. "Well sure, go with Batman if you want the easy reference, I thought about it, but it was low fruit so I went with the Spidey one."

He laughed. "You know, you don't seem overly in awe at my little ball of light here."

"This is Serenity, weird stuff happens here all the time. You'll have to do better than that if you want to impress me, Mr. Wizard."

"Fair enough. Scoot over, I need to look through this blighter's pockets." He knelt down by the robber and started going through his coat, reaching inside he stopped, pulled a small plastic baggy out with something that looked like sticky tar inside and held it up for Hannah to see." Do you know what this is?"

"Not really," she said. "But I'm guessing Nancy Reagan would want me to say no if offered."

"That's pretty close. It's called majeesh, it's a supernatural drug, gives mortals access to the magicks for a while along with an enormous high. On the flipside, magic folk get wicked powerful for a couple of hours and higher than a good chunk of the audience were at Woodstock."

"So, mucho bad mojo then. Good to know," she said

"Yeah, and on top of it, the stuff's like Red Kryptonite with humans, you never know what's going to happen."

"Now you're just trying to impress me with the comic book talk."

"Is it working?"

She smiled at him. "Maybe a little. What about this guy? He wasn't doing anything I'd call supernatural? Just another loser with a gun."

"Looks like he was almost out, that little bit wouldn't last more than 10 minutes or so, and the garbage is super expensive. I'm guessing he was looking for an easy victim to rob so that he could buy more. But he ran into you instead, poor bastard."

"How'd you show up so conveniently anyway?" Said Hannah.

"Majeesh gives off a signal, like a supernatural warning sign. When it comes to magic it's practically radioactive. I can track that and follow it." Holding the baggie, he said, **"Ignis perdere."** A flame in the palm of his hand engulfed the tiny bundle, a moment later only ash was left. He dusted his hands off and gestured at the robber. "What about him?"

"I was going to tie him up and leave him for the cops."

"Let me." He held out his hand and touching his middle and ring fingers to his wrist he whispered something in Latin **(Araneae Vintum)** and then loudly said, "THWIP." Spider webs shot out from his wrist, wrapping the robber in a cocoon, then flicking his fingers, the wizard lifted him into the air and attached him upside down to a fire escape, dangling him high above the pavement with a thick line of webbing.

"O---kay, that was pretty impressive," she said.

"You going to leave a note?"

"Nah, figure I'll call the cops and tell them where they can pick him up.--- Tomorrow morning. After he gets really cold and has to pee super bad. Because justice."

An awkward silence passed between the two of them, Hannah fidgeted and began to look over at nothing in particular. "I better head home," she said. "Probably going to be in trouble anyway for staying out too late and saving doctors and talking to strange boys." She closed her eyes and mentally berated herself a moment for being a spazz. She blurted out, "My name's Hannah, y'know, in case you were wondering and since you didn't ask."

"I should go." He paused for a moment and looked directly into her eyes. "If you want answers, meet me tomorrow night at the Pirates football game." He smiled and winked at her, and walked away.

"That's not weird at all!" She yelled after him. "Why the football game?"

"My Spidey-Sense is tingling." He called back.

"Cool," she said out loud to herself. "Wait! What's your name?"

The wizard vanished. "Merlyn."

*****

Hannah gently opened the window to her upstairs bedroom and silently snuck inside. It was pitch black and she stumbled over a pile of books on the floor that made a loud bang as she made her way to the lamp beside her bed. *Oh crap*, she thought, *I hope mom didn't hear that.* Immediately upon turning on the light she froze and her heart caught in her throat, Hannah's mom was sitting on the edge of her bed.

"Hi sweety, you're grounded." Her mom scrutinized her with equal parts amusement and exasperation. Hannah, while wearing a sheepish grin was simply happy that after being so late her mother wasn't yelling at her in the dreaded mom voice, the one that isn't raised but seems louder than a crowd at a soccer match.

Sarah Harrison was a beautiful woman; small with a slight frame, in her late thirties with long blonde hair highlighted by wisps of silver, and strong enough to pick up a car and throw it down the street. Like mother like daughter, super strength ran in the family. "We had a deal," she said. "Home by 10 o'clock on a school night. Particularly the first school night."

"So not my fault," said Hannah. The excitement in her voice was infectious as she paced back and forth telling her mom about how she saved the family and how thankful they were. How good it felt being hugged tight and admired by the little boy and how she left the robber tied up for the police. She left out the part about the wizard boy though, telling your parents everything when you're seventeen is universally impossible. "And obviously I should not be grounded and you should probably make me pancakes for breakfast in the morning before I leave for school." Summing up her night's adventure like a lawyer's closing argument she stood there with arms folded and with serious if not hilarious intent.

"Well, I suppose if you were all busy fighting for truth, justice, and whatever I guess grounding you isn't quite the correct teenage management response." Beaming with pride she got up and hugged her daughter until she heard her say, "ouch."

"Jeez, mom, super strength hug much?"

"You can handle it, kid. But please be careful, I know we've trained, I know I can't stop you and probably shouldn't, but take small steps. There are things in this world you are not ready for yet. If something ever get too dangerous, you call me immediately."

"I will," said Hannah. "This was only a scummy mugger though, I can totally handle a jerk like that." Her mom flashed her an irritated look. "I promise. I'll be careful."

"Okay, good talk, now go to bed. You need to be up early enough to eat pancakes." Her mom walked over to the bedroom door and paused for a second. "Something else?"

"I met a cute boy." Hannah felt embarrassed but she was excited and wanted to tell her mom so she continued anyway. "And get this, he's this badass wizard with really cool white hair and a scar over his left eye. Like Harry Potter except way more of the After School Special bad boy type."

"So he helped out?"

"Yeah. Well kinda, and mostly after everything was over. But he did this cool Spider-Man thing."

"I'm glad you met a cute boy and thank you for telling me, but remember, be careful. When it comes to magic and this town, not everything is always what it seems. If you're going to be part of all of this you have to know that."

"And I do. Really. It was just some harmless flirting, that's it. Besides, it was nice to meet someone a little like me."

"Okay, lecture over," said Sarah. "So what was magic boy's name?"

"Merlyn."

"What?"

"Um… Merlyn."

13

For a moment Hannah thought she saw her mom's expression get a whole lot darker but she wasn't sure. "Ah," she said. "Night, sweetheart."

"G'night, mom" A second after her bedroom door was closed Hannah's thoughts were racing. *What was that about? Who are you, Merlyn?* She pulled out her phone and started searching for information on wizards named Merlyn. There was a ton of information, most of it was the usual pop culture Arthurian stuff, old guy with magical powers and a beard mentors a new king, fights witches, turns into a squirrel, things like that. A few obscure references from Germany and Britain portrayed him as a particularly nasty manipulative jerk, and couple that she found she was pretty sure were online posts about someone's D & D character, some were contradictory and more than a few were just plain weird, but in almost all of them there was a common myth about him. "The hell does 'age backwards' mean?" She said aloud. Sleep remained elusive that night and even when she did nod off it was so restless and full of turmoil that it could hardly be considered sleep at all.

*****

The twisted man descended the old stone stairway into the catacombs beneath the city. Down he climbed, dragging his left leg and supporting himself with a crutch. Surrounded by the wet and the rot, he held a piece of cloth over his mouth and nose to stifle the sweet smell of decay. But he coughed and wretched anyway, this place wasn't meant to be travelled to by the living. Ruinous tunnels stretched for miles under the city, winding and turning, sometimes stopping without warning, in fact there was another entire city right below the one above. A century ago the earth shook and swallowed it whole; the streets, the buildings, the people, this place had become their tomb. Only the dead were left here now.

Reaching the bottom, the twisted man found himself on an old street paved with stones, mostly cracked and overturned. Gas lanterns recently lit lined the street and illuminated the buried city block. He looked up at the brutes following him down the stairs and called to them. "Hurry up," he said. "We were supposed to get there over an hour ago." Three creatures trailed behind him carrying large sacks filled with human parts and pieces. They were large and grotesque patchwork monsters towering over seven feet tall each, they moved slow and deliberately, and they smelled of antiseptic. Bones stuck out here and there where they poked through the sacks. None however were without the flesh still attached, these people pieces were fresh and removed from the recently dead.

At the end of the street they reached an old building with the lights on inside, it had been a church before the quake. Two stories tall and made of brick it had a large metal cross on top that had remained intact and the building itself was surprisingly sound with a slight lean from the crumbling of the foundation over the past century. The twisted man and the brutes entered the church through an opening where a rotted wooden door hung mostly to the side off its hinges. They walked between two rows of church pews to the front where a man in surgical scrubs worked on a body laying on a concrete slab. He was covered in blood and surrounded by machines and sharp instruments; the machines whirred and wheezed, pumped out smoke and belched, and glowed red and green in the darkness. Analog masterpieces, as much created from sorcery as science, they seemed alive.

Lowering his surgical mask the man spoke to them, "You're late, Samuel."

"I apologize, Doctor, some of the parts you requested were harder to find than others."

"But you found everything?"

"Yes."

"Good, I'm pleased. You three," he said, pointing at the brutes. "Put our new arrivals in the coolers. Then go sit down. " Several large meat coolers were lined along the side of the room next to the pews and plugged into generators, the brutes took the sacks over and began taking people pieces out, stacking them like steaks from the supermarket. When they finished they sat down in the pews where another twenty dead things sat as well, these weren't as big as the brutes but they were more vicious. Zombies. Sitting and staring, falling apart from rot, sometimes groaning a little.

"Did you get the other things I asked for?" Said the doctor.

"What? Oh, yes, right over here." Samuel limped over to the coolers and picked up a large sack that hadn't been opened, he turned it upside down and dumped out two dozen football jerseys along with helmets onto the ground. He picked up one of the jerseys and brought it over to the doctor, lucky number 7.

The doctor held it up against the light of the machines with his bloody hands. He smiled wide, showing his absurdly straight white teeth. "Go team," he said.

Chapter 2: The Gang's All Here

Morning sunlight illuminated the Harrison home, quiet stretched throughout the neighborhood…and was immediately shattered by Hannah backing her car out of the garage and hauling ass down the street on her way to pick up her friends before school started in 30 minutes. The Hannah-Mobile was a silver 1968 Volkswagen Karmann Ghia 2 door coupe with red leather interior and a 6 speed manual transmission. Ever since watching Mike Myers drive around San Francisco in one while wooing 'Harriet, sweet Harriet, Hard Hearted Harbinger of Haggis' in 'So I Married an Axe Murderer' it had become the car of her dreams.

To no surprise, it was also her favorite movie, *love and murder always go so well together in the pictures,* she thought. "When I grow up I want to tell stories about people in love and turmoil," she'd told her mother once.

"Is there any other kind?" Her mom responded.

All during her tweens and early teens she had saved her money to buy a Karmann Ghia, when she turned 16 a year and a half ago her mom had matched those saving and they had gone searching for her baby. Although not the easiest of cars to locate in their neck of the woods they found one at last rusting out in an old farmer's junkyard about twenty miles outside of town past the Toth County line. It was faded orange like a basketball left out in the sun too long and more upholstery was gone than remained but to Hannah it was the most beautiful car in the world.

Most of the repairs and restoration Hannah taught herself how to do, she'd even installed a new 6 speed transmission herself over the past summer. While working on it her mom had commented that she was the type of person who didn't want to reinvent the wheel but instead wanted to drive as fast as she could on the best tires around. The new silver paint and red leather interior had been made possible by saving her holiday and birthday gifts over the past year and a half and by teaching self defense courses at the local YMCA. And now he was finished and oh so pretty. She called him the Silver Surfer.

Hannah came to a stop in front of very nice house in a very nice neighborhood, one of those Stepford Wives neighborhoods where everything is too perfect and everyone looks like they're about to do something awful to break up the boredom. An attractive girl with long black hair wearing a green shirt and white shorts raced out of the house towards the car, she had an expensive looking purse, a backpack with maybe one book in it and was wearing a pair of shoes that likely cost more than Hannah's new transmission. Kiran Amanat, faithful fantastic friend since the first grade and the craziest most straightforward person in Serenity.

"So what do you want to do?" Asked Kiran as she climbed into the pretty silver automobile.

"I want to hit the bitch with my car," said Hannah.

"Not the Silver Surfer," Kiran exclaimed. "Let's go steal something much bigger and then hit the bitch with that."

"Good plan, we need a vehicle of sufficient enough size to make her go splat." Hannah grinned as she accelerated down the street, her baby purring like a kitteny badass. "Is Matt okay?"

"He says he is but I know he's devastated. Seriously, only child and his parents disown him for coming out. The hell is wrong with people?"

"Creepy religion is what's wrong, Lisa was awesome until she found Jesus," said Hannah. "Matt's dad's always been a surly goon so there's no shock there, the religious nuttery just strengthened the goonery." Hannah paused. "Where's he staying? Does he need a ride today like you other transportation deprived deadbeats."

Kiran laughed, "You just became your mom, Han."

"Shush, you."

"Nope, he's staying with his cool aunt that Lisa and George hate. She only lives a few blocks from school so he's good to walk." Said Kiran. "And you know, I wouldn't have to be a deadbeat if daddy would buy me a new car."

"Maybe you should stop wrecking them," chided Hannah.

"Not my fault," protested Kiran. "All of those other drivers and trees and ditches were plotting against me."

"Oh, I'm sure."

Hannah took the next corner sharp and fast entering the rundown old neighborhood, continued half a block and then pulled into a driveway three houses down on the left hand side where the pavement was cracked, chipped and falling apart throughout. She came to a stop outside a modest single level home that had been built in the 50s; it was well kept up on a block where few were, the lawn and gardens that surrounded the home were spectacular, the dirt beds were filled with enough flowers to impress a floral monger and the aroma was sweeter than the words of a poet.

A slight pretty girl wearing a yellow sun dress decorated with red and pink roses growing along a green vine along with a white sweater exited the house and walked toward the silver car, she had short pink pixie hair and wore large black glasses that seemed too big for her face, her arms were full of books that kept slipping out onto the ground and she wore a backpack shaped like a stuffed Yoda getting a piggyback ride. Her name was Cassie Marcos and they had all been friends since forever, or least since second grade when she'd moved to Serenity with her dad after her parents' divorce; she was quiet, beautiful, bookish, the smartest girl in school, and a secret hellion when surrounded by her friends. When she got to the car Kiran jumped out and leaned the seat forward so that she could climb in the back.

"Did you forget any books?" Asked Kiran.

"I don't think s....shut up." Said Cassie. A big grin came across her face and all three of them burst out laughing as Hannah sped away at an unsafe velocity. "I missed you two delinquents."

"So how was your mom and life in the big city of Wichita?" Asked Hannah.

"Good, as controlling as ever. Can't stop talking and thinks that any opinion not her own is some kind of challenge. It's always funny when the quiet person says something the loud person doesn't like, you'd

think a bomb had gone off. The recrimination is usually immediate and it is almost always self serving in the guise of altruism."

"Quiet, you? That's silly talk." Said Kiran.

"Darn right," said Cassie. "I'm not quiet, I'm just choosy about who I talk to and what I say." She sat forward peeking between the front seats. "Mostly I just missed my dad, it's nice to be home. So what did you two do while I wasn't here to keep you safe and sane."

"I met a cute boy last night after saving Batman." Hannah exclaimed.

"Wow, way to fail the Bechdel Test there, Han." Kiran replied. "And break the fourth wall, I guess."

Hannah side eyed her friend. "The Bechdel Test is stupid." She recounted last night's adventure for them in lush detail, paying as close attention to the cute boy traits as she could remember and emphasizing the particular satisfaction she felt knocking out the bad guy.

"He's a wizard?" Said Cassie.

"Like a Harry Potter wizard or a Gandalf the Gray wizard?" Said Kiran.

"Um, both I guess, except hot and our age. I think," said Hannah. " His name's Merlyn."

"As in King Arthur?" Asked Kiran.

"Maybe," said Hannah. "Weird thing is that the stuff I found online last night said he ages backwards, whatever that means. But this guy didn't look old or even act old, he was making Batman and Spider-Man jokes."

"Oooh, maybe he ages backwards like Robin Williams in that show," said Cassie. "He's like Mork from Ork."

"How the hell does that work?" Kiran said.

Hannah hit the dash in mock frustration. "He's not like Mork goddammit. Don't ruin this for me."

Cassie made a rude face at her from the back seat. "Whoops. So very sorry." She paused for a second. "Mork, Mork Mork Mork."

"God this town is weird," said Kiran. "Well good, maybe he can help you not get killed playing superhero."

"Aw, I didn't know you cared, mom," said Hannah.

"Shut up. Just because I act like I don't care doesn't mean I don't think you're nuts. Please be careful, Cassie and I don't have time to break in a new Powerpuff Girl this year. You're our Buttercup."

"Thought I was Blossom, but okay, whatever." She paused. "I will, I promise. Can't explain it but I know I have to help people, and it's not because I should, it's because I can."

"Saint Hannah, protector of the people. Well, I suppose that has a pretty decent ring to it." Said Kiran.

The Silver Surfer glided into the school parking lot about five minutes before the start of class, Hannah parked him as far away from the other cars as possible, turned off the ignition, and leaned back a second before getting out.

"Listen, Merlyn wants to meet up later at the football game, now I'm not completely eighteen and naïve, I want all of you there with me."

"Date or danger?" Asked Cassie.

"He says his wizard sense is tingling, sounds like something bad is on the way."

"Typical start to a new school year in Serenity. We'll be there, Han." Said Kiran.

Hannah and Kiran turned and looked in the backseat as Cassie tried to organize her books enough to get out of the car. She grinned. "Sidekicks assemble!"

*****

Merlyn was eating a late lunch in the old observatory's living quarters when he heard a loud pounding at the front door. Setting his bologna sandwich back down on the plate he went over to see who it was, *salesmen or missionaries most likely*, he thought, no one knew he was back in Serenity, and anything too nasty would have set off the mystical alarms he had cast around the place. He blinked in recognition as he peered through the peephole at his old friend on the other side, he undid several locks, some physical, some mystical, until he opened the door and greeted his visitor with a wide grin. "Huntress, long time no see."

The woman standing there was far from happy to see him, she made a fist, cocked her elbow back, then stepped forward and punched him square between the eyes, eliciting an unfortunate and decidedly loud noise from the wizard. Then grabbing hold of his belt she lifted him off of the floor and tossed him to the other side of the room where he landed on top of a long wooden table where he had been eating dinner, plates and cups crashed to the floor, breaking and spilling across the room. After a moment Merlyn rolled off of the table and onto the floor where he crouched on his knees to gather himself, he let out an almost silent moan and braced his hand behind his lower back where he'd impacted the table the hardest.

Eyeing his assailant he croaked out a couple of words amidst the gasps of pain. "The hell, Sarah?"

Sarah Harrison moved up next to him and after pausing for a second kicked him in the stomach, sending him doubling over, struggling to breathe. "Why did you contact my daughter?" She asked.

"Ugh, Christ, calm down a second. You want an answer or do you want to keep kicking my ass?"

"Honestly, I haven't decided yet," she said. "Better talk fast or I might get bored and hit you again."

"I needed to see what she was like, supernaturally speaking this place is lit up like the sun right now." Merlyn gingerly climbed to his feet, wary of being hit again, and sat down on a soft leather couch a few feet away from an old soot covered fireplace. "Every sign and portent in the western hemisphere says that something big and bad is about to happen here. I need allies, and since you're out of the game I had to see if she was ready to fight."

"You stay the hell away from her, she isn't some soldier to be drafted into your schemes," said Sarah. "Neither one of us are anymore."

"Don't give me that nonsense, you know better. The fight doesn't just end because you say it does. None of this stops while you call a time out, it just goes on and on until the next group of kids comes along and picks up their sticks and stones, and then it starts all over again with new faces and new players." Merlyn paused, picked up a slice of apple that had landed on the couch and stuffed it in his mouth, then continued. "That's the horrible truth, you know, your lot's curse. Deep down you're all a hell of a lot more like Cain bashing his brother's brains in than you are like sweet Abel." He leaned back, crossing his arms and putting them behind his head, his brown eyes growing darker, wider, and more malevolent. "Besides, you two aren't exactly sitting out on the sidelines playing spectator. You've been training her. No one starts off that good, you sure didn't."

"Of course I have, but not for you to use and manipulate, I did it because it had to be done. For her sake." Sarah eyed him with suspicion. "If you need someone to fight your stupid battles then I'll do it, leave my daughter alone."

"Sorry. Can't." said Merlyn. "It has to be her."

"You are not honestly trying to sell me, of all people, some 'Chosen One' line are you?"

"Course not, I went to see The Witch of Wichita a few days ago, and she says it has to be Hannah. Or else she'll end up dead at the end of all of this."

"The hell do you mean, dead?"

"The witch's words, not mine, she isn't exactly linear these days."

"You went to see Allison?" Asked Sarah.

"I did. By the way, she says hi."

"Is she alright?"

"More or less," said Merlyn. "Crazier than the last time you saw her but otherwise okay. She moonlights as a patient at an asylum outside of town, I think that's a cover for her coven. The inmates are literally in charge of the nuthouse."

"And she said that Hannah will die?"

"Yeah, it was a genuine prophetic warning from your old bestie. Guaranteed."

Sarah thought about what the wizard had said for a minute and then continued, "Alright, I won't get in the way. But I'm warning you, take care of her, and if anything happens, come get me. I won't let you use her for whatever all of this turns out to be."

"Believe it or not I plan on protecting her with my life. Nothing will happen, you have my word."

"And we all know how much that's worth, don't we?" Sarah sat down in the comfy reading chair facing the fireplace and the couch, she regarded Merlyn with disdain. "David never did like you, you know. Alison and I, we did, and we trusted you, but not him, you never had him fooled." Before he could reply Sarah pressed the wizard for more answers. "What is this wicked hullabaloo that's supposed to hit anyway? Any of the usual suspects in the lineup?"

"No, all that the seers and the witch could say was that Hannah needed to be out on the frontlines and that we were dealing with the

mystical equivalent of an atom bomb that was about to go off. Oh, and that chaos and death would follow."

"So, it's just like old times then," said Sarah.

"Pretty much."

Sarah nodded, got to her feet and started for the door. Merlyn followed. "Keep her safe."

"I will," he said. "Oh, and Sarah," Merlyn leveled a sinister gaze at her and raised his right fist, the room grew cool and dark, his eyes became black as night. "DO NOT FORGET WHO AND WHAT I AM.... I may look like one of you but I am not." Sarah began to grab at her neck and was lifted off of the ground as if being raised by an invisible noose, she fought to breathe but there was nothing around her throat to fight. Merlyn opened the door with a snap of his fingers and with a swatting gesture threw Sarah outside onto the lawn surrounding the observatory, upon impact the invisible force around her neck was released and she gasped for air. "Remember that lesson the next time you drop by on an old friend."

The door to the observatory slammed behind her and Sarah thought to herself, *Maybe I shouldn't have kicked him while he was down. Oh well, he's a jackass.* She stood up, wiped the grass and dirt off of herself and walked over to her car, as she got in she took out her cell phone and dialed a number to somewhere in Germany, waited through a particularly long (and German) techno song until at last someone answered. "Hannah needs your help."

*****

Matt kept clicking the Zippo lighter open and close over and over again, it was chrome with a marbled rough texture and an inscription on it that read, "Amor Nec Imperari Potest," translated it meant, 'love cannot be commanded' in Latin. His aunt had given it to him the day after his parents kicked him out of the house.

Classes had ended half an hour ago, he sat inside an old red boxcar by the school track where the football team stored their practice equipment, his head resting against the cool metal wall. A flame danced along his fingertips as he held the pipe to his lips and lit another bowl of majeesh, he brought the heavy smoke deep inside his body and after holding it a moment exhaled slowly through his nose and mouth. This was the last of it and he wanted to savor the effects for as long as possible.

Through the cracked door a breeze stirred the dust inside and caused Matt to wrinkle his eyes, he held his hand in front of his eyes and saw that his fingers were missing, a bird of prey's crooked talons had replaced them. For a moment

29

he stared at his new appendage, unafraid and bold with curiosity, and then he realized his eyes were sharper as well, his hearing too. He gazed through the narrow opening, seeing farther and fuller than ever before, and he listened to his new world for the first time.

Nature had never been a passion of Matt's, he didn't have anything against the outdoors but had always figured that it and he were both best left alone by one another. This was different though, he felt more like a part of it than before, a participant as opposed to a spectator. He could hear the grass crunch beneath someone's feet as they walked towards the boxcar, angry that he was about to be interrupted and fearing discovery of his secret vice, he closed his eyes and tried to force the magic away. Some things once beckoned are hard to get rid of, in his mind he pushed back against a giant eagle that sought to overwhelm him; the struggle continued as the bird ripped at his flesh, leaving him bloodied and beaten, at last flying away as he lay huddled and sobbing on the ground, becoming a tiny dot on the horizon of his consciousness.

When he opened his eyes everything was back to normal, his surroundings were duller, the colors and sounds more muted than before. His hands once again had five digits but they ached from the transformation; he wiggled his fingers, felt them crack and pop from the stiffness, as if breaking in a new pair of gloves. Kiran opened the boxcar door, sliding it over on its rusted wheel and groove, making an insufferable racket, and stepped inside. The bright midday sun was too harsh, Matt covered his eyes with his t-shirt and lowered his head, Kiran said something to him but he couldn't understand it, her voice had been drowned out by too many new sensations, and she smelled like honey and limes. Subtle magic is even harder to get rid of than a powerful spell, it lingers on the skin, in the hair, and in the recesses of the subconscious; the Id is its own sorcerer.

"What the hell are you doing?" Asked Kiran. "It smells like the shittiest of vape rooms in here."

Matt took his head out of his t-shirt and grinned at her like a fox, "Vaping's for wusses, dear girl." Then he moved back and banged his head on the wall of the boxcar.

"Hey! Stop that."

"Can't, gotta get it out. Gotta stop."

"Jesus, you are high," she said. "Come on, let's get you home." She bent down to help him up and taking the empty plastic baggy and pipe she stuffed those underneath a tackle dummy laying on the floor. "Anymore contraband?"

"Nope, but I'm coming back for that pipe, it looks like the Starship Enterprise."

"Oh, this pipe?" She took it out from beneath the dummy and smashed it with the heel of shoe.

"That's mean."

"Tough."

They left the boxcar walking close together and she squeezed his hand, "You're going to be okay, you know. We all love you."

31

"I know, I'm just kinda really fucked up right now. I'll get over it," he said. "It's my mom, you know, dad was always an asshole but at least I could count on her. I had a plan. I didn't expect all this."

"Thing about plans is that they suck. Sometimes you have to just float on the wind and end up where the current takes you."

"Damn, that's wise stuff, Kiran."

She laughed, "Your fault, I must have gotten a contact high back there."

Chapter 3: The Monster, The Mother, and The Maiden

The monster burst through the stained glass ceiling of the old church and fell upon his foes. Shards of blue sky and yellow sunlight cascaded down, pieces of broken angels tumbled from their lofty perches onto those below, and the rapturous faithful were soon scattered to every corner of the sanctuary. The monstrous man was massive, seven feet tall with three foot shoulders, hands the size of hams, his feet were larger than a tennis racket, and he was dead. Black streaks accented his mostly gray hair but his skin stood out, it was bleached white, like polished ivory stone. He wore a dark gray button down shirt with rolled up sleeves, black cargo pants tucked into black army boots, and crisscrossed over his back were a broadsword and a battle axe, along with a Russian Kalashnikov strapped across his chest hanging to the right.

Beneath him the marble floor had been broken apart and removed to the sides, revealing the earth beneath it, a half dozen men with weapons, dressed like soldiers surrounded a deep pit excavated in the middle of the church. The monster slammed into two of them with a righteous force, driving them into the ground with a satisfying thud. They were modern day knights belonging to The Order of the Anti-Saint, Clovis Lapierre; devil worshipping Knight Templar of the Second Crusade and all around insufferable sorcerous prick. Underneath the church there was a reliquary containing several of his body parts; having been chopped apart by an angry Parisian mob in 1789 for crimes against the people, members of the Catholic Church had taken it upon themselves to bury the pieces across Europe to prevent his followers from reassembling his corpse and restoring him to power. *Apparently this lot does not give up easily,* thought the monster.

Upon setting his feet firmly on the ground he seized the nearest knight, tore off his head and tossed both it and his body into the pit. Then wielding his battle axe he charged the other three, despite a hail of bullets the monster tore through them like tissue paper, landing blow after blow until little remained of the men who had stood before him a moment ago. One of the knights he landed on had survived the impact and was attempting to reload his rifle. As he flung the last evil knight against a brick wall, causing multiple bone breaking sounds and audible human suffering, German techno-pop began to play from the monster's cargo pants' pocket. Reaching inside he grasped a large smart phone that was putting on a raucous light show and answered it. "Guten Tag," he said in a much more cheerful voice than you would expect from creature of his size and bearing.

His features became heavy and concerned, and as he listened he tapped his large fingers against the pommel of his axe. From across the Atlantic more trouble had found him, as it always did, centered in the Convergence no less, bad mystical happenings in that place were like normal Thursdays everywhere else. He recalled the first time he'd set foot in Serenity, it had been in September 1905, the land surrounding the town had looked like the golden fields of Elysium, or they did until Malvolio and Caledon set them ablaze. The two wizards had battled each other with such a horrific appetite for destruction that the resulting earthquake buried most of the old city. He'd never known who the victor was, there only seemed to be the lost and the dying afterwards. The whole weekend had been one catastrophe after the next, at least the second time he was there no natural disasters had taken place, although supernatural disasters could not be helped. Perhaps the third visit would be better. *Doubtful,* he thought.

"I will be there in a few hours," he said. "Have faith, we will help your daughter, she will be alright. Auf Wiedersehen." He paused, listened, and then let out a deep belly laugh. "Ja, fur dich, I will change my horrible ringtone before I get there. See you soon, Sarah."

As he put his phone away and began to clean his axe with a cloth from one of his pockets the doors to the sanctuary swung open and a priest walked in followed by two armed men, members of the Swiss Guard but minus the bright colors and wearing modern day suits. He was a young priest in his mid-thirties; tall and skinny, fit, had light brown hair, and wore jeans along with his black shirt and white collar and appeared to be at ease amongst the carnage. His eyes gave him away though, they were dark, and his face was lined with worry in a way that no man his age should be. "Is the reliquary safe?" He asked.

"Here." The monster opened a large crate next to the dead knights stuffed with straw and an aged steel box wrapped with chains and locks. "Either they didn't have time to open it or they were ordered not to."

"Most likely the latter," said the priest. "They would want to gather all of the pieces before beginning. This is a good thing, so far they only have an arm and a leg. Did you leave any alive to question?"

"That one there," pointed the monster to the man collapsed against the brick wall. "Although perhaps for not much longer."

"Ah, yes. Well, we will be quick about it then. And we will move the reliquary to a safer location. Again. Thank you for your help, my friend."

"Always," said the monster. "Father, I must get to America as soon as possible. Is the church's Cessna X available?"

"For you, Karl, always," said the priest. "I will have it fueled and waiting within the hour at Charles de Gaulle."

"Danke, Henri," said Karl to the smiling priest.

"You so rarely call me that that I sometimes think you have forgotten."

"Not forgotten. You are simply so much taller than the boy who used to steal apples from my trees that it often eludes me for a moment."

"Hmm, life is change I suppose," said Henri.

"Yes. Life is." Karl stood there a moment and looked over the carnage, determination in his gaze. "I'll leave you and your friends to clean up. Be well, father." The monster's strides were long and heavy, within seconds he was outside and climbing into a custom made vehicle that didn't look street legal and resembled one of those monster trucks that performed for redneck audiences in the states. Dirt and mud kicked up ten feet into the air and the roar of the engine sounded dangerous and deep as he sped off to Paris and the Charles de Gaulle airport.

"May the lord bless and protect you throughout your adventures," said the priest. "Be safe, my dear friend."

*****

Shorty's Saloon was a hole in the wall dive located on the wrong side of town, it was on the corner of a two story red brick building that had been built about a century ago; some of the bricks were crumbling, the green paint on the sideboards was peeling, and the window glass looked perpetually dirty. The place had seen better days, and at the moment everyone inside except for Shorty and Sarah Harrison were unconscious and lying on the floor, or across the tables, or even sticking out of pinball machines in various states of beaten up. Shorty himself was screaming, nailed to the wall through the left shoulder with a pool cue, a pool cue that Sarah Harrison kept tapping further and further into the wall with her index finger. Bump bump bump.

"I'm disappointed in you, Shorty, I thought we had an understanding. I let you run your little cons, do a touch of bad here and there, but nothing serious, no one gets real hurt and no one gets real dead. Good for you, good for me, good for America. I figured you'd at least come to me if something or someone particularly wicked showed up. And now I hear there's an apocalypse in town, and I haven't heard a peep from my good friend Shorty. Now why is that?"

"I didn't know. I didn't know. I would have told you if I'd known, I swear. I'm sorry." Shorty whimpered and sobbed as Sarah twisted the pool cue deeper into his shoulder. "Please, I didn't do anything wrong."

"You know something," she said. "Nothing happens in Serenity without you getting a whiff of trouble. You're a connoisseur of evil stink, Shorty. Spill or I start on the other shoulder, least now you can still tend bar and wipe your own ass."

"Okay, there's something, but I didn't think it mattered."
"Tell me."

Shorty cleared his throat. "There's a body thief in town," he said. "Some cripple being followed around by two big brutes, they've been raiding the morgue and funeral homes all over town this past week."

"And you didn't think a body thief was worth mentioning to me?" Sarah said. "The hell is wrong with you?"

"Hey, creepy creatures do creepy things all the time. I figure they're already dead, what's the harm, not everybody and everything are looking for a hug, y'know."

"Ew. I'm gonna forget I heard that last part. Where are they taking the bodies?"

"I don't know, I swear." Sarah whacked the pool cue with the side of her hand, eliciting a deafening scream and more crying from the little bartender. "Sweet fucking Cthulu! He yelled. "Fine. I don't know jack about crap for sure but word is they're being taken down below, into the old city."

"Super, my favorite place," said Sarah. "Now what about the majeesh that's in town, who's selling it and where's it coming from?"

"The Berserker's been selling it out of a restaurant in Little Scandinavia called Odin's Beard." Shorty said. "And that is all I know, I godsdamn swear it."

"You gave up that last bit easy enough, you're not setting me up are you?"

"No way, that majeesh garbage is bad for business, all these junkie freaks start running around town like they're the baddest of the bad, disturbs the norm and people and creatures stop hitting the town for their evening cocktail."

"Alright." Sarah ripped the pool cue out of the wall and Shorty slid down to the floor crying. "Thanks, Shorty, you've been a peach."

Sarah decided to follow up on the majeesh lead first, the timing was too much of a coincidence, the two somehow connected, how she had no idea, but a quick drive over to Little Scandinavia was a lot easier than searching the ruins beneath the city. Now all she had to do was deal with the Berserker, and she hated that guy, everyone did.

On the drive over Sarah couldn't help but think about what she had done almost twenty years ago. The Berserker was a leftover from the old days when the demons and the monsters still ran the city, before Sarah moved to Serenity during high school. Back then he was a middle management lieutenant for Magnus Von Magnusson, a minor fire demon from Muspelheim who escaped sometime in the 12th century and went on to create a criminal empire based on herring and murder. The Berserker himself wasn't actually a Norse Berserker or a demon or an immortal or anything supernatural at all, he was human. Just a big man that liked to hurt and kill people who worked for an even bigger jerk that liked to do the same. Osfrey Swierczinski was his actual name, he got his nickname by flying into rages and leaving behind piles of bodies, Magnus Von Magnusson had given it to him, he figured a name like that would frighten his enemies and friends alike. Despite all of that he was still the lesser of two evils, and it was Sarah Harrison's fault that he had been the devil in charge of Little Scandinavia for almost the past two decades. He was a monster but a least he was a manageable human monster.

Sarah and her friends and allies had fought the forces of evil in Serenity for years to small avail, nothing really changed, except that the people she knew and cared about kept dying. So she made a plan and she made some deals, and one night eighteen years ago, 'The Long Night' Allie had called it, they battled the monsters and the demons until they were either dead or banished from this reality. Nothing and no thing had escaped. But in order to get rid of all of the big fiends she'd to make a few deals with a couple of the little fiends, this did two things, it got rid of the big bad supernatural bastards and it filled any power vacuums, preventing a war for control later on. *The world will always be full of evil,* she thought at the time, *but maybe that evil can be controlled a little.* She had regretted those compromises for nearly the past twenty years, but they'd worked, for the most part Serenity had become a peaceful place to live, almost normal. The Berserker had been one of those compromises, with a little supernatural help he betrayed and killed Magnus Von Magnusson, and in return for his cooperation and agreement to keep his affairs strictly human he got to be the gangster in charge of Little Scandinavia with no interference from Sarah Harrison or her allies. An agreement that he was now breaking. *But why change things? What's happening in Serenity now that doing this would benefit him?*

Thirty minutes after leaving Shorty's Salloon Sarah pulled her old Waggoneer into a parking space half a block away from the entrance to
Odin's Beard. An old wooden sign hung outside the door to the restaurant, carved in the shape of a man's beard and goatee, it was painted white with a dark outline and had the restaurant's name inside of it in black lettering. The building itself looked like an old Scandinavian wooden lodge with a

fake thatched roof that rose to a high inverted vee shaped point and a half wall along the bottom made of stone. It was all made new to look old.

Sarah grabbed a bastard sword out of her back seat, got out of the car, went down the block and stepped into Odin's Beard; it was like walking into an opium den that smelled like licorice, fish and shit. A cloud of smoke drifted throughout the place; cigars, cigarettes, vapes, and majeesh; they all blended together into one noxious barf inducing smog. Opera played in the background, something by Wagner but not the usual movie music; customers ate dinner, drank at the bar, and all around she could see little acts of magic as a dozen or so people smoked their pipes full of majeesh; thaumaturgy and trickery, the place was full of chemical warlocks dressed like extras in a Norwegian gangster flick, mob goons and junkies bristling with temporary supernatural powers.

With sword in hand Sarah walked right into the middle of the restaurant, and no one paid her a second glance, they were either too high or else a woman with a large sword was so far down on everyone's list of weird sightings for the day that they couldn't be bothered to look. She peered over the busy crowd and found the Berserker, he was sitting at a table in the back surrounded by his lieutenants and handful of beautiful women, prostitutes and hangers-on. He was a giant of a man, all muscle and no neck, he had long silver-white hair, a big snowy beard, and he wore a white suit with a black shirt and black tie. An ornate pipe with the bowl carved like a bird of prey's talons holding it, rested in his right hand as he laughed loudly at something, smoke curled out of it and towards the ceiling, whether it was majeesh or tobacco she didn't know.   Strewn about the table were liquor and leftovers; vodka, herring, and majeesh; baggies and joints, pipes and bongs. Sarah Harrison had ventured inside to confront a den packed with dangerous gangsters turned warlocks, so she did the sensible thing, she walked up to the Berserker's table, slammed her bastard sword down on top of it, spilling their booze and drugs everywhere, looked him in the eye and said, "We need to talk."

The Berserker smiled at her, his teeth were as large and white as his stupid outfit. "Hello, Huntress," said the evil gangster. "I've been expecting you to stop by."

*****

"Let go of my mother," said Hannah. She stood at the threshold to Odin's Beard, the door wide open behind her, the bright sky outlining her silhouette. The crowd inside turned and looked, bewildered at the young girl standing there nonchalant, chewing her gum, blowing bubbles and seeming at complete ease amidst the cacophony. She sauntered inside with her hands in her jacket pockets, moving her head this way and that, her long dark hair falling in front of her eyes, taking in the scene; tables were overturned, glasses were broken all over, food was on the floor, frightened customers huddled underneath tables, and a handful of evil junkie magic minions were crackling and smoking with nefarious mystical power, ticking time bombs. And back by the bar the big bad Beserker and two of his juiced up lackeys had her mom pinned down on a pool table, the Beserker was holding her own bastard sword at her throat.

"What are you doing here?" Said Sarah. "And how did you find me?"

"I pinged your phone," said Hannah. "Wanted to borrow twenty bucks for the game tonight but when I saw that you were here I thought you might need some help."

"That's sweet dear but as you can see I have everything well in hand." Said Sarah.

"Oh, I'm sure," said Hannah. "I'll just hang out, you let me know if you want any help."

Sarah Harrison winked at her daughter and then kicked the bastard sword out of the gangster's hands into the air, tossed the two lackeys holding her onto opposite sides of the restaurant and flipped herself into a crouching stance on top of the pool table. She caught the sword in midair and decapitated the Berserker in one fluid swing. As his body fell it slumped forward before hitting the floor and his head rolled onto the table. "Eightball, corner pocket," quipped Sarah.

"Oh my God," said Hannah. "That was so awful it was great. You should be ashamed of yourself."

"I am." Said Sarah. She glanced at the astonished look on the Berserker's face and then turned to crowd in the restaurant. Most of the people had run out the front door when she killed the gangster but a half dozen chemical warlocks were on their feet now and getting ready to attack either her or Hannah.

An idea popped into Hannah's head so she spoke up, almost shouting. "It occurs to me that there's a position open for crime lord of Little Scandinavia, so instead of fighting us and most likely losing and almost certainly ending up dead, you guys should fight each other. Winner becomes the new king." The warlocks turned on one another faster than either Sarah or Hannah expected, the room ignited in a mystical struggle for power and position. Fire engulfed the bar and wind spun the tables from one side of the room to the other as mother and daughter ran for the exit.

Before she was out Sarah yelled back at the combatants, as they momentarily paused she said, "And have no doubt, when it comes to the boss of bosses in this town, I'm the one who's in charge. Whoever wins answers to me. No more majeesh. No more magic. If you break those rules you join the Berserker." With that said she slammed the door shut and joined her daughter down the street by the Silver Surfer and her SUV, the fight inside continued as it shook the entire city block. "With any luck the idiots will wipe each other out," she said to Hannah.

"Hey, mom, I know the Berserker was a first class evil meanie but I thought we didn't kill humans."

"We don't. You don't. Ever." Said Sarah. "He'd turned himself into a warlock and I made a one time exception to fix a mistake of mine from a long time ago." She paused. "And I'll pay for what I did today, eventually. But something ginormously bad is brewing in this town right now and we have to stop it."

"How do you know?" Asked Hannah.

What her mom said next surprised Hannah. "Because Merlyn Morningstar is the harbinger of bad news. He's the damn chaos bringer. Wherever and whenever he shows up, trouble follows."

Morningstar. Hannah let that sink in for a second. "You know him?"

"Yes. You need to be careful. Merlyn always has a plan, and he'll do whatever it takes, no matter who get hurts, to see it through."

"Okay then. What do you want me to do?"

"Go to the game, if he says there's trouble then there will be. Save as many lives as you can while I try to figure out the source of all of this craziness. Luckily the Berserker got a little chatty when he thought he had me, whatever's going on up here has its beginnings below the city."

"Will do." Hannah was about to leave when her mom grabbed her and gave her and big superhuman hug. "Oof," she said as she felt like a safe and snuggled little kid again.

"I love you so much," said her mom. "Be very careful…and DO NOT trust that wizard. He's on our side…but just barely."

"I will, mom, you be careful too. I love you." As Hannah drove away she watched her mom wave until she turned the corner. The sun was still bright but it had started to go down in the west, purple and pink highlighted the sparse clouds that floated through the sky, it was evening, almost game time, and she had a wizard go see.

Chapter 4: Prelude to a Nocturne

A column of flame as tall as a man hung suspended in the air, its sinuous red and yellow bands spinning and twisting together like a double-helix, the shadows it cast on the walls moved and flickered, as if they were a story on film being projected onto a screen. Silhouettes of agony reflected around the room for the wizard to witness, suffering foretold and forewarned by an angry parent. "My son," said the voice from inside the fire.

"Dad," said Merlyn. "I'm a little busy, what do you want?"

The fire grew and so did the voice, it filled the observatory, consuming but not burning. "You should silence your voice before it is silenced for you."

Merlyn put his hands in his pockets and began to whistle as the flames fell over him, "Oh, but so many have died for less, and I do so love to hear myself talk." He twirled his finger in a 'whatever' gesture
and held out his hand, the fire in the room collapsed into a sphere no bigger than a baseball resting in his palm.

Now diminished, the voice from the fire continued, "I worry for you, the events and powers you have decided to oppose here exist outside of our domain, what will happen we cannot see."

"Yes, wouldn't want to screw up the plans for your bouncing baby Anti-Christ, would we?" Said Merlyn. "Good talk, I'll try to remember to send you a card and a neck tie for Father's Day, preferably a noose. Bye, dad." He blew the fire out and dusted the ashes off by clapping his hands back and forth. Despite the unwanted interruption it was a beautiful night in the observatory, the domed roof was open and the stars were beginning to shine in the early dusk sky, a crescent moon was overhead, it's luminescence shining beside the few clouds travelling through the atmosphere.

The observatory was filled with arcane items and work benches scattered throughout, a veritable maze of secondhand magical junk; on one table near the telescope a book with a dark red leather cover lay open for anyone to see with a page devoted to skin removal curses, on another table a blue-ish liquid sphere filled with white light floated above a golden statue of a forearm with an outstretched hand, near the door to the apartment a mummy from South America was propped against the wall, its death shroud deteriorating, rictus teeth grinning, and sitting on the floor next to a half assembled wooden coffin were two Chinese butterfly swords, one with a red phoenix etched onto it the other with a green dragon. Off in a corner below a tapestry of a medieval battle attached to the wall rested an old green army footlocker flecked and faded from age, Merlyn opened it and pulled out two white drumsticks carved with symbols and spells, looked them over, then shoved them into his back jeans' pocket.

Snatching a light weight brown jacket off of one of the tables, Merlyn put it on over his black t-shirt, grabbed the butterfly swords, stuffed them with the hilts sticking out into an old army backpack laying on a table, flung it lopsided over his right shoulder and left the observatory. For a moment he lingered as he reset the protection spells that guarded the place, a subtle red flash appeared and faded as he finished and began to leave. He walked down the path behind the buildings, away from the road, curving around trees and bushes, descending the hill towards the town and the school. Searching through his coat pockets he found a soft pack of filterless Chesterfield cigarettes and an old brass lighter with a red pentagram on it that a warlock had given him at Berkley in '68. Lighting his cigarette he recalled an old Johnny Cash ballad, *Mean as Hell,* and started to sing.

> *The Devil in Hell we're told was chained*
> *A thousand years he there remained*
> *He neither complain nor did he groan*
> *But was determined to start a Hell of his own*

"Oh Johnny," he said aloud. "You ol' rapscallion you." And he laughed and sang louder and louder and the night became darker and all the bad folk got ready to come out and play.

*****

The stadium lights flickered on as Hannah climbed the bleacher steps to her friends, Kiran and Matt, who were waving to her from about halfway up on the fifty yard line. She was wearing black yoga pants and a red zip-up hoodie with a Robin logo on the left breast, her shoes were green Chuck Taylors and she had a collapsible baton hidden up each sleeve. When a wizard says badness is afoot you best come prepared. A sudden gust of wind chilled her to the bone as she climbed the steps, so she threw her hood up over her head and stuffed her hands in the kangaroo pockets, how Kiran was managing in shorts and a t-shirt was beyond her, at least Matt had the decency to wear khaki pants and a gray sweater. Upon reaching their row of bleacher seats she dashed over to Matt and picked him up with a back breaking squeeze. "You big doofus," she said smiling.

"Good to see you too, Han," he said through clenched teeth.

Hannah held on to Matt and hugged him almost as hard as she could, popping his back and causing him to let out an audible groan. "We love you, you know," she said as she loosened her grip. Matt shook his head that he understood and Hannah let him go. "And no more of that crap, okay?" Matt glanced at Kiran. "Don't blame her, I would have known soon enough anyway. That stuff is really bad. Seriously, this is Serenity, you don't play with questionable magical items here. Remember?"

"I know, I know," said Matt. "I won't anymore, I promise."

"Cool, now while you detox off of the bad mojo one of us will keep an eye on you 24/7. Cool? Cool. Not that we don't trust you but we totally don't trust you right now." Before Matt could say anything else Hannah looked at Kiran. "Hey, where's Cassie?" She said.

"On her way," said Kiran. "She texted me a few minutes ago that she was just leaving the house."

"Bet she dyed her hair again," said Hannah.

"Probably," said Kiran. "After all, you know who will be here, all jocked out and ready to play some Monday Night Football."

"She needs to give in to the pitter patter of her heart already," said Hannah." Zeke's hot, and smart, and nice, and he likes her. She's gonna miss out if she doesn't stop over thinking things."

"Yeah, no doubt. They're like really good looking brainiacs in love, their super children could probably rule the world someday. It would be totally adorable if it wasn't kinda barfy."

"Cassie and the hot football guy like each other?" Said Matt. Hannah and Kiran stopped, turned to the side, and gave him an epic WTF look, and after a moment of silence the three friends began to get the giggles. "Guess I have been really out of it lately."

"Welcome back to Planet TMZ," said Hannah.

"Heard the term 'salted weasel' today," said Matt. "Not sure if they were referring to an animal thing, a food thing, or a sex thing."

A large fit of laughter came over everyone again and lasted for minutes until they were all out of breath. "You are so random!" Said Kiran.

"Yup, and that is why you all love me."

They watched the field being prepared below and the spectators fill the stands while they talked about nothing important at all for twenty minutes until Cassie arrived. She'd colored her hair bright blue and was wearing red Capri pants along with a tight black tee that featured a tooned up jolly roger on the front; she was also wearing 3-inch cheetah heels which Hannah figured must have taken some kind of supernatural power to climb the stadium stairs with. As soon as she made her way over to them she sat down and immediately took them off. "Ouch," she said. Everyone grinned at her discomfort and commented on her cute outfit, but only Kiran passive aggressively mentioned her looking good for a certain football player, which she ignored with a not so subtle glance the other way.

"So is wizard boy here yet?" Asked Cassie.

"Not yet," said Hannah. "And oh dear lord do not call him wizard boy…. please. I don't want to completely piss him off on the first date." Everyone looked at her funny. "Fine. Horrible monster fight. Whatever. He's probably literally a hundred years old anyway. Stupid creeper magic."

"I'm just glad we're all here to help you….um, fight off evil I suppose," said Cassie.

"If the words 'beat off' and 'first date' get mentioned here in the next minute, I'm leaving." Said Kiran. There was a moment of quiet and then everyone began to shake their heads. "Geez, tough crowd."

"Oh my god, we're a gang now," said Matt. "A monster fighting gang. How cool is that?"

"Oooh, we should have a name for our gang," said Cassie.

"Let's go with group or league," said Hannah. "Gang makes it sound like we shake down little old ladies for spare change and hard candies."

Everyone else's voices seemed to become smaller and further away as Hannah watched Merlyn approach through the side entrance of the stadium near the outlet to the foothills. He walked like he couldn't be touched, with a self assurance gained by conquering enemies from without and from within. *Lord almighty, Mr. Merlyn, if you aren't just the handsomest devil I've ever seen,* thought Hannah. *Momma warned me about boys like you.*

*****

Merlyn clicked his tongue against the roof of his mouth and pointed at Matt, "You're part Indian." Silence answered the statement as Matt flushed with anger and anxiety.

"Merlyn, dear," said Hannah stepping between the two. "We say Native American now. Kiran's the one who's Indian, y'know, because she's actually from India."

Kiran had an annoyed 'why me' look on her face. "Well technically I'm Pakistani but whatever, us Desi folks just look the same to you people."

"You people?" Said Hannah, mock indignation dripping off each syllable. Kiran grinned and the awkwardness was interrupted by laughter as the two couldn't keep a straight face.

Merlyn glanced at the two, clearly irritated. "Blame it on the time travel," he said, "the vernacular always changes on me."

"So that's what 'ages backwards' means, huh?" Hannah said. "You're a time traveler, which is really pretty cool. Good to know. Past or future?"

"Both, and it's not like I have a Tardis," he said. "I'm a chronomancer, I use the temporal magicks birthed during the apocalypse to journey throughout the key mystical eras of mankind in an attempt to prevent the end times."

"Wow," said Hannah. "That sounds....kinda crappy and lonely actually."

"Yeah, it's a real hoot," he said, then raising his voice to Matt, "Well, are you or are you not part Native American."

"Yeah, my grandfather was Navajo. What of it?" Said Matt.

"That's good," said Merlyn. "Now I won't have to magically kick your ass."

A dangerous mask fell over Hannah's features. "Walk soft, wizard boy," she said. "I don't care who, what, or how good looking you are, if you threaten him again I'm the one who'll have to kick YOUR magic ass."

"Sorry," said Merlyn backing away. "But I can sense it, he woke something up within himself by using the majeesh." He paused and addressed Matt again. "You've been shapeshifting, haven't you? When you use the drug. It was most likely simple sensations at first, your senses were heightened, like an animal's, and then you'd start to become one of them. And now they're in your mind as well. Am I correct?"

"Just the eagle today." Matt paused. "And before that there was a wolf about a week ago whose fur it took me a day to get rid of."

"And are they still there, in your mind? Said Merlyn. "Can you still feel them clawing at the corners of your thoughts trying to get back in."

"Yeah. Guess I didn't think about it until now, but they're still there, I can feel them trying to get back in." Said Matt.

"You opened up a big door into the Witchery Way, kid, and now we either need to shut it or make sure it doesn't knock you on your ass as you walk through."

"The hell's the Witchery Way?" Asked Matt.

"It's old magic, tied directly into the earth," said Merlyn. "Very powerful. Navajo shamans use the connection for all sorts of things. Some good. Some bad. On the bright side of things you can be equal partners to the power. On the dark side though you could become the power's puppet. You were on your way to becoming a skinwalker."

"That sounds bad."

"Think werewolf or wendigo, you become a thing the beast controls. An evil thing. And skinwalkers are the worst of the worst, basically a demon jumps your spirit and takes you for a ride."

"So you're going to be my Obi-Wan Kenobi?" Said Matt.

"Sure, for a bit," said Merlyn. "Just don't get me killed in the last act, kid. We'll start tomorrow, important evil shenanigans are still ahead tonight." Kneeling, he picked up the backpack with the swords and handed it to Hannah. "Those are for you. Drop the batons in the bag, they won't be enough tonight, major badness is on the way." He looked at her with an amused expression. "Wizard boy?"

"You were being a dick," she said.

"That's the problem with you people," he said. "No one says anything important anymore because you're all too afraid of offending each other. Be brave, Hannah Harrison, piss off someone you love today."

"Great advice, I think I'll start with you."

"Aww, we just met and you already love me, I'm flattered."

Hannah shook her head and then motioned to the contents inside of the bag. "What are these anyway? Aside from beautiful and pointy."

"They're called 'The Celestial Twins,' the Dragon Blade and the Phoenix Sword. Story goes they were forged with sacred steel by a shaolin blacksmith during the Boxer Rebellion and blessed by a thousand monks who could never speak again afterwards. That's all bullshit of course, they're ancient, created and enchanted by the same guy that made Excalibur, and your mom's warhammer." Merlyn's hand brushed against Hannah's for a moment as he handed her the swords. "I

picked them up at an estate sale in Lubbock, Texas a few years ago, thought they might come in handy."

"No way the same guy made these that made freaking Excalibur! So cool! Exclaimed Hannah.

"The very same. What'd you expect? After all, my name is Merlyn."

"Wow," replied Hannah. Then, tilting her head to the side, "So how you do know my mom?"

"Ah, figured she might mention me," said the wizard. "We go way back. Benefits of travelling throughout history, I get to meet all of the major players in their prime."

"Hmm, gotta say, she's not your biggest fan, wizard boy."

"Stuff happens when you fight the big, the bad, and the ugly. Not all of it's nice, she has good reason not to like me, you should listen to her." He clapped his hands together. "But for now I come bearing gifts, check out the swords."

"You are not what I expected, Mr. Merlyn, and I still can't decide whether that is a good thing or a bad thing." Hannah examined the swords inside of the bag. "They're amazing," she said. "like the perfect accessories for the monster hunting girl on the go."

"Thought you might like them. Supposedly they can't be broken and they lend the user courage and heart." Said Merlyn.

"Throw in a brain and it sounds like they were made by The Wizard of OZ."

"You never know, I hear Baum dabbled."

The levity of the moment was interrupted by a cacophony of screams from down on the field, a pack of zombies dressed in football uniforms rushed into the stadium and were attacking a group of cheerleaders near the away team's goalpost. In the stands the crowd was yelling and stampeding down the steps and over the seats in a mad exodus to safety, causing as much damage to each other as any zombie likely would have. Hannah's friends were terrified as well but to their credit they stayed put and were waiting to hear from her what they should do.

Hannah broke the gang... league's silence. "Holy shit."

"Yeah, those are zombies alright," said Merlyn.

Chapter 5: Team Zombie

"Oh crap, we're all going to get turned into zombies," said Matt.

"Don't be silly," said Kiran. "We'll probably just get torn apart and eaten."

Merlyn eyed them with disdain. "That's actually a common misconception perpetrated by the current societal fascination with the undead. In fact, zombies don't infect, they're only reanimated corpses, probably being remote controlled by some dick necromancer."

"Well that's good," said Hannah. "And dang, you do love your epic Wizardsplaining."

Merlyn pursed his lips as if he intended to say something and then thought better of it. "They still crave human flesh though, so watch out for that." He said.

"Super."

"But they're totally dead, kill the hell out of them. Have a party."

She looked closely at Merlyn, "Watch them. Please."

"I will. Now go, do your superhero thing."

Hannah held up the twin Chinese butterfly swords he'd given her, inspected them, sighed, and then ran off towards the disaster unfolding on the field. The zombies were everywhere. They had already killed a couple of cheerleaders and were now descending on the band and the home team. On the visitor's twenty yard line one of the monsters was strangling Nelson "Bro" McClonsky, the team quarterback. Hannah cut the thing in half at the waistline, its legs immediately dropped and its intestines and guts spilled out of its mid-section. The beast however would still not surrender, despite being cut in half it continued to wrap its hands around the quarterback's throat and squeeze until his neck broke. Cursing the thing in language her mom would probably chew her out for Hannah cleaved its head in two, right down the middle. She glanced down at the dead quarterback. "Sorry," she said.

One of the zombies began attacking the spectators in the stands, fearing she couldn't get there in time Hannah picked up a discarded javelin lying in a pile of track equipment and launched it at the monster. After sailing across the field it struck the zombie in the head, puncturing its brain right through the hole in the side of the football helmet.

"Damn, nice shot," Hannah said to herself.

Merlyn glanced over while getting the other kids to safety. "Damn, nice shot," he said to himself.

Several minutes of fighting went by and either by accident or act of God the P.A. system started playing *You're the Best Around* (from Karate Kid) as Hannah shoved a butterfly sword between another zombie's eyes, through its brain and out the back of its football helmet. Two more of the creatures grabbed her from behind; she elbowed one, knocking its helmet off and causing it to fall, and then swung with her free sword, severing the second zombie's head. Blood spurted out from its neck stump, spraying her before the headless body toppled over. Sticky with fresh gore she dislodged the other sword and drove it through the head on the ground, piercing the brain. As the zombie fallen got up and came towards her, Hannah slashed both swords in front of her in an X motion parallel to the ground, slicing the top of the zombie's head off right below the hairline. Its body dropped immediately, the brain spilling out in separate top and bottom halves, and the skullcap rolled away like a dinner bowl.

More of the creatures came at her, directed by their faceless puppet master to abandon their victims and eliminate the girl who was spoiling all of the carnage. Hannah was about mid-field and completely surrounded by over a dozen zombie football players, she raised both swords in a Shaolin Boxing Monkey fighting stance…and noticed something odd. The green dragon and the red phoenix were glowing slightly, and she could hear music; subtle Chinese string music, it was lovely, and amid the terror, completely calming. "Okay, you dead jock bastards, *bring the noise.*"

*****

The kids were panicking and out of breath as Merlyn shoved them into the announcer's booth. It was a small solid building made of red brick with uneven mortar that had dripped through the cracks and along the side, a heavy steel door was the only way in or out, and the windows were high enough that they would be hard to breach and crawl through. It was a place that could hold off an attack by zombies for a good long time.

Kiran's frosty blue eyes locked onto Merlyn's, "You don't have to leave us here," she said. "We can go with you or you can stay with us."

"We really can help," said Cassie. "Hannah needs us, she can't do this alone."

Matt kept wringing his hands and feeling through his pockets, looking for the drugs that were no longer there. "Oh Jesus, those were actual freaking zombies out there?" He said. "What are we going to do? What are we going to do? What are we going to do?"

Kiran snapped her fingers at him. "Focus sweety, you're rambling. And stop that," she said as she held his hands in hers.

Merlyn looked at her sympathetically. "You can help the most by staying out of the way and by keeping your tasty brains safe."

"Oh Shatner," said Matt. "That is so gross and insane to think about."

"But what if they come after us in here?" Said Cassie.

"Follow your cable television training and go for their heads. Now close the damn door and barricade it behind you. And play some music for Christ sakes, every fight scene needs a soundtrack."

When the door closed Merlyn raised his arms and muttered an incantation, his hands turned red and flames flickered along his fingertips. He grasped the door handle, melting it, then ran his palms over the outer edges of the door, making it hot and molten until it was fused to the building. Hoping that would be enough to keep the kids safe he hurried back towards the field where he saw Hannah fighting off undead after undead creature. Merlyn stopped, stood still and closed his eyes, he turned his head to listen to the carnage and to the wind; for a minute he stayed there and did only this, and then he took off like a bat out of hell towards the parking lot.

Dusk settled over the asphalt and the cars, the streetlights flickered above casting and recasting the ominous scene, and everywhere, the shadows danced. Merlyn stopped running when he reached the lot; he walked by row after row of cars, peering inside, looking underneath, around and over, desperately trying to find the boss at the end of the level. Halting at a rusted out old Chevy pick-up he closed his eyes and began smelling the air, almost immediately he detected something foul, a spiritual odor of sorts that reeked of death and perverted life. Something wicked was hiding in the school gymnasium.

As soon as he stepped foot into the gym three large brutes charged at him; they were massive patchwork fiends stitched together from several bodies, their skin was sallow and they smelled like rotten meat. When the first one lunged at him with outstretched arms all he could think about was that he was being attacked by the Universal Monsters version of The Three Stooges. *Nyuk nyuk nyuk*. Whoever cut their hair had not been kind.

Planting his feet, Merlyn prepared himself for Moe's mountainous embrace, as soon as his meaty hands wrapped around his throat he took

hold of both of his arms and tore them off of the creature. Stepping back he began swinging them like a pair of 80s state fair nunchuks and then sprang forward to beat the hell out of the other two stooges. Moe collapsed onto the ground, dark fluids rushed out of his arm stumps, his sorrowful half life leaking away. Larry and Curly retreated back into the gym, their mouths agape, shocked at what had happened.

Merlyn discarded Moe's arms and reached into his back pocket, grabbing a pair of drumsticks. They were both about a foot long, bleached white and carved from bone with dark symbols etched into the surface. Egyptian hieroglyphics, Babylonian cuneiform, English, French, Chinese characters and a dozen or more languages were written precisely in tiny script all over the bone wands; these were wizard weapons, charged with enough arcane power to level an army. The wizard raised both of his arms, pointed the drumsticks at the creatures and spoke in a booming voice. **"ANNIHILARE!"** They both exploded as if something had detonated inside of them.

In the hallway up ahead a small man supported by an old crutch walked towards him; he had sandy blonde hair, wore ill fitting clothes, and had a twisted left leg which he had to drag along. Though pieces of the brutes were all around the corridor the carnage didn't appear to bother him; he was muttering something beneath his breath that sounded like a chant and he kept looking all around as if expecting something to happen.

"Now who the hell are you?" Merlyn asked.

"Sssamuel," said the twisted man.

"Right. Okay, listen flunky, just take me to your leader and no one else needs to get hurt or blown up. Sound fair?"

"Sssuck it, wizard."

"Well that's not nice. I mean, damn, I know you're evil and all but I'm going feel like a right jerk beating up on a handi-capable minion of darkness."

As Merlyn's words trailed off the twisted man stopped and began to shake, his teeth rattled in his skull so loud that the wizard could hear them from ten feet away, color drained from his face and his bones cracked and popped as his skin stretched and grew over his expanding figure. His hair fell from his body and his nose fell off, his skin became hard, scaly and leathery, a forked tongue darted out of his mouth and his eyes became cold and serpentine.

The wizard was transfixed, standing there so close to him was an ophidian; a snake man, a demon creature from old nightmares that had preyed on human beings before the written word had been invented. Dragon Men. *Okay, these things are supposed to be dead,* he thought, yet here it stood, and its name was Samuel.

Smoke drifted from the Dragon Man's nostril slits and from the corners of his mouth. He leaned forward, elongating his neck toward the wizard and opened his jaw, showing dozens of large needle shaped fangs and the emerald light of a supernatural fire rising from the gorge of his belly. They stared at each other for a long while until Merlyn gave the Dragon Man a cocky blink; the beast stepped forward and looked at him with malicious glee, then with a roar unleashed a torrent of prehistoric napalm death onto the wizard. The fire acted like a living thing, its bluish-green flames behaving as if they were the fiery jelly tentacles of a

hellish octopus, they reached and grabbed at Merlyn, slithering their way around him until they enveloped him completely. Upon stopping, the creature pulled back to admire the too-beautiful sight of the arrogant little mage writhing in agony and perishing in front of him. Unfortunately for him the wizard wasn't screaming.

Standing there in singed jeans and a t-shirt smoldering from the Dragon Man's fire Merlyn burst out laughing. "Oh, Sally, I crap better black magic than that." Gesturing absently with his wand he sent the ophidian smashing through the concrete wall and over the parking lot until he landed unconscious in the empty lot across from the gymnasium and the football field. This was no time for revelry and self congratulation though, a serious countenance fell over his face, *after you defeat the nasty minions and arrive at the end*, he thought, *you've got to beat the boss to level up.*

As Merlyn entered the basketball court he could feel the unholy evil of necromancy being used, the darkest of magicks. To use that kind of black magic was an abomination to the natural way of the universe; things were born, they lived, and they died; deviating from that path was dangerous, and the consequences were often unexpected and severe. Magically speaking, the place reeked.

Located about mid-court was a tall athletic looking man with dark hair and a full beard, he wore a well tailored charcoal gray suit with a white shirt and a black tie, his black shoes were polished to a shine and he had an old silver watch on his left wrist that was attached with a cracked and faded tan leather band. He stood before a great machine turning dials and pulling levers; a ten foot tall, five foot wide analog obelisk ripped from the dreams of Jack Kirby and Stanley Kubrick. Merlyn had never met the necromancer and mad scientist before but he immediately recognized him from description and reputation; Doctor Victor Frankenstein, corpse stealer, maker of monsters and immortal villain.

Summoning as much ambient voltaic energy from the surroundings as he could Merlyn clasped his hands together and channeled a firebolt through the Bonham drumsticks, sending it crashing towards Doctor Frankenstein and his machine. The lights in the gymnasium went out and all that could be seen was the flash of the lightning bolt as it travelled across the basketball court. And then the unexpected happened, without turning away from his machine Doctor Frankenstein extended his left arm and caught the bolt in his hand, for a moment he kept his arm outstretched but as the glow faded and the lights in the gym came back on he resumed his tinkering on the device. To

Merlyn's astonishment and irritation, after several seconds of silence the doctor started laughing.

"All that pretentious build up and then nothing," said Doc Frankenstein. "What was that you said to Samuel about crap magic? Sorry, I couldn't help but overhear your clever banter out in the hallway."

Merlyn gathered his wits and stared directly at the famous mad scientist, *well that didn't work,* he thought, *so what the hell is Plan B?* "Touché, asshole." *Maybe I'll just piss him off until he gives up.*

"Did you know you smell like death, little mage? Apparently you've spent some time on the other side of the curtain." Frankenstein stopped what he was doing and gazed at Merlyn. "How did you manage to come back here? In the entire history of the world that has only happened a time or two. What makes you so special?" Pausing, he raised his hands and muttered a curse. "Doesn't matter, all dead things are play things to me."

Something began to tug at Merlyn inside, an invisible hand had taken hold and was attempting to drag him along. "Screw this," said the wizard. Pointing a wand at the ceiling above, he shouted, **"PERDERE!"** A crimson flame shot out of the drumstick, blasting an opening fifty feet wide that shook the whole building. Debris rained down on Frankenstein and the machine, the doctor screamed and cursed at him as he attempted to shield the device, and a cloud of dust settled throughout the gym.

When the smoke cleared, the obelisk and Frankenstein were nowhere to be seen but Merlyn could feel that another spell had been cast by the necromancer before he disappeared. More dead were rising out by the football field. The people killed by the first group of zombies were now zombies themselves, only these weren't being controlled, they would be completely berserk and only interested in feeding. Merlyn dashed out of the gymnasium and towards Hannah as fast as he could.

*****

Hannah finished off the last zombie football player with a forty-five degree arc from the phoenix sword that went through the helmet, bone and brain, in one fluid movement. Despite the carnage and being covered in enough gore for a half dozen splatter movies she couldn't help but smile a little at that last one. It was a brief reaction, as she looked over the football field the horror of what had occurred began to set in.

Bodies in various states of dismemberment were strewn throughout the field from goal post to goal post, the grass was torn up from the fighting revealing the earth beneath, and the bleachers were falling down in large sections. For the most part Hannah wasn't bothered by the majority of this, she'd been fighting and training with her mom since she was little, Sarah Harrison had prepared her little girl for the world's secret supernatural wars. Taking zombies apart and being covered in blood wasn't the problem, seeing people she knew dead on the ground was. "No battle is without its innocent victims," her mom had warned.

Most of the crowd attending the game had fled but not all, scattered around the field were a dozen victims of the monstrous attack, about half of which she recognized. There was Nelson "Bro" McClonsky, the team quarterback who she didn't like and couldn't save, and over by the sidelines there were two blonde girls, sisters and cheerleaders that sat in front of her during Algebra last year, they had both loaned her their notes when she had missed a week with the flu, they were so nice but try as she might she couldn't remember their names. Hanging from the top of the bleachers was Mr. Wright, her sweet old history teacher with the wispy white hair and the funny name, one of the zombies had torn out his insides which were lying on the ground below. Over by the entrance was Mrs. Yost, her Girl Scout den mother leader lady who kicked her out when she eight because she'd argued that thin mints were making Americans fat. Her skull had been caved in before Hannah could get to her. And then there was Rob Marsden and Katie Summers, everyone's favorite all-teen all-too-much PDA high school couple, at least they looked like they'd been killed making out over by the refreshment booth. "Stupid asshole zombies," said Hannah.

A cool breeze quickened onto the field and the stadium lights flickered, the tiny hairs on Hannah's neck stood up and goose bumps crawled over her arms. The blonde cheerleader sisters were the first of the newly dead to get to their feet, they ran towards her, an ear piercing shriek accompanying them the whole way, like a cheer from a banshee.

"No no no," said Hannah. "Not you guys too, how is this fricking fair? Come on." She hit the first sister in the side of the head with one of the swords, knocking her over, the second one she kicked in the right shin, snapping the bone and causing her to collapse. Meanwhile the rest of the recently deceased had gotten up and were also coming at her. Hannah retreated to the visitor's goal post and reluctantly steeled herself for another fight, she raised the phoenix sword in her left hand towards the closing zombies and held the dragon blade down to her right side for a counter blow. And in her head she listened again to the blades' song.

Without noticing somehow Merlyn had appeared right next to her. "Hey," he said, sounding cocky and full of himself. "Want some help with these guys?"

Hannah looked at him and said with relief in her voice, "Please. I know half of these folks."

Merlyn looked at her. "Makes it harder," he said.

"A lot harder."

"I'll finish it." He said. Stepping away from her, Merlyn raised both of the Bonham drumsticks to the sky and started to speak in a loud German accent. **"EIS. ATEM. STURM GEHORCHT MIR."** Then continued in English. **"FREEZE THESE MOTHERF*****S!"**

Dark clouds gathered above, lightning and thunder shook the ground, and the temperature dropped way below zero. Hannah lost sensation in her fingers but she could feel how charged the atmosphere had become with electricity. She watched as Merlyn conducted an orchestra of ice and wind, he moved his hands in graceful sweeping arcs, directing the storm to each of the zombies, leaving them as solid ice, unmoving statues frozen in place. And as the cold consumed the last of them he snapped his fingers, calling down the lightning, shattering the undead and spreading their icy pink parts across the field.

For a moment Merlyn stared at the sky whispering something, a moment later the clouds departed and the temperature began to warm up again. Feeling too tired to stand he leaned against the goal post and looked at Hannah, to his surprise he didn't quite get the reaction he expected.

"Why the hell didn't you do that in the first place?" Hannah asked, exhaustion and exasperation hanging on her every word. "You could have saved these people from the start, goddamn it."

For a moment anger crept into his voice. "Listen. This kind of an environmental spell comes with a cost, all magic does, something like this will leave me weakened for days." He paused. "And I needed to find the necromancer." Merlyn stopped before saying anything else and lowered his eyes. "I'm sorry."

"What was that?"

"I said I'm sorry, you were right, I should have done this first."

"Well at least you admit it."

"None of it mattered anyway, somehow he could counter my spells. Made me feel like I was in my first year at Hogwarts." Hannah's eyes lit up a bit at that. "Um, no, sorry, there's no wizard school. Not yet anyway."

"Damn," she paused. "You're a tease. Silly time travelling wizard boy." She started wiping the blood off of her face with the sleeve of her hoodie. "Who was is it anyway?"

"Doctor Frankenstein."

"No. Way."

"Seriously. Guy's a first class necromancer and crazy pants mad scientist. He was doing something with a weird machine that looked like it belonged more in 2001: A Space Odyssey than Buffy The Vampire Slayer. I think he's feeding it the chaos from events like this, probably the same a-hole distributing the majeesh around town."

"So he's the big bad? I thought the doctor was the good guy. What about the monster in the movies?"

"From what I hear the monster's a hell of a guy, real champion for the forces of good. Turns out Mary Shelley's book was more unauthorized biography than work of fiction. She just turned the good guy bad guy roles around to make it more appealing for Romanticism era readers."

As Hannah thought about what Merlyn had said the two stood there not knowing what to say next, without alarm or sense of urgency they both noticed the snake man lying across the street in the empty lot rise to his feet. After a quick look towards them he ran off down the block disappearing from sight. "Shouldn't we go catch him?" Hannah asked.

"I wouldn't worry about that guy, pretty sure he got a negative score on his SATs. Besides, I traced the doc's disappearing act, I think he's holed up beneath the city. We'llget ready and then go help your mom, who I'm guessing is way ahead of us."

"She is."

"Good, we'll need to prepare now that we know who we're up against."

Hannah looked at him funny. "God you're man-splainy." Then, after a second she went over and surprised him a soft kiss on the lips and put her arms around him while resting her head on his shoulder. "Now I'm sorry, that was rude, I really am glad you're okay." She pulled back but reached for his hand, holding it lightly. "Where's everybody else? Are they all okay?"

"I put them in the announcer's building and then sealed it up, even the big bad wolf couldn't get in there."

"Ah," said Hannah, a relieved smile lit up her face. "So that's who was playing the fight music. Big surprise, Matt's had a crush on Ralph Macchio since the second grade."

As they walked over to the cinderblock building one of the Pirate football players ran up to join them. It was Zeke Collins, star running back, math genius, super nice guy, handsome fella (according to Cassie) and all around winner of the genetic lottery. "What the hell was all of that?" He asked Hannah. "And when did you become Xena? And Who's Iceman... er, Storm here?" He said pointing at Merlyn and looking utterly confused.

"Sorry, Zeke." She put a hand on his shoulder. "Magic's real and there are monsters everywhere. Welcome to my world."

"Oh, okay." Zeke paused. "Well thanks for saving my life, I guess. Mind if I walk with you guys?" He stared down at his feet. "Um, is Cassie okay?"

Hannah smiled, she knew that Cassie and Zeke had liked each other ever since last year in Calculus. Silly smart kids. They were both totally chicken about doing anything about it though, which would have been adorable if it wasn't so frustrating being their all knowing all seeing go between. "She's fine, we're going to get her, Kiran, and Matt right now. Come on."

Once they arrived at the cinderblock building Merlyn pointed at the magic welded door, "You mind?"

"Nope," said Hannah. " Feats of strength are one of the Festivus requirements."

"Wow. And she knows her Seinfeld, I might be in love," said Merlyn.

Squeezing her fingers into a couple of places where the door wasn't melted to the wall Hannah took hold of the door and tore it off its hinges, tossing it ten feet away. Inside her friends all gasped and then laughed as they piled on her into one big standing group hug.

"Thank Willem Dafoe as Jesus—you're all right!" Exclaimed Matt. "And we're okay too, which is even better. Are all the zombies gone?"

"They're gone," said Hannah, a touch of sadness in her voice.

Backing away from Hannah, Cassie noticed Zeke standing there, without warning she wrapped her arms around him and planted the greatest whiz bang kiss of her life on his lips. "Um, hi," she said. "I'm glad you're okay."

"Hey, you," he said, a bit shocked. "Me too."

Hannah and Kiran looked dumbfounded at what had just happened, "It's always the quiet ones," they said in near unison, and then exchanging glances started laughing so loud it echoed out into the evening air.

"We need to go," said Merlyn. Everyone stopped and looked at him, listening with intent. "This may not be over yet, we have to get somewhere safe and figure out what to do next."

"Where do you suggest?" Asked Hannah.

"My observatory."

"The creepy old place on the hill?" Said Hannah pointing at it. "That's your place?"

"Yeah, it's warded against all sorts of nasty stuff."

"Okay, sounds like a plan. I'll drive my car with Cassie, Kiran, and Matt. Zeke, you have a car, right?" The running back nodded. "Good, you take Mr. Wizard and lead the way. Better if the two people here with superpowers aren't in the same car."

A gloomy demeanor came over the group after their celebratory reunion, they all set off towards the parking lot without saying anything else. Merlyn recovered the gym bag from the bleachers that he had brought the swords in, and taking a long white cloth out he tossed it to Hannah. "For the swords," he said. "It isn't good to leave them stained with cursed blood like that. Hurts the magical bindings." She started polishing the swords, first the ruby etched phoenix sword and then the jade etched dragon blade, they were both magnificent, the gore easily came off and they glowed in the moonlight, the only different thing about them now was that she could no longer hear them singing.

Hannah felt exhilarated from the fight, her pulse and breathing quickened, she became flushed from her face down to her chest, and she could feel the blood flow to the center of her body. Up by the gymnasium and the parking lot Merlyn walked alone, he'd kicked off what was left of his shoes and his feet were bare, his jeans and black t-shirt were singed, falling apart and clinging to his lean frame, he had the Bonham drumsticks stuffed in his back pocket. She could smell his sweat, his strength, and the shampoo he had used on his hair earlier in the day, he was intoxicating.

Close behind him followed Cassie and Zeke, the new couple, exhausted and leaning next to one another as they shuffled off of the field, their hands clutched tight together for comfort and reassurance. Cassie whispered sweet things in Zeke's ear, private promises she thought only he could hear, but Hannah could hear too and she laughed a little to herself how bold the quiet girl was when she thought no one else was listening.

Directly ahead of her Kiran and Matt walked at a slow pace without saying a word to each other, Matt looked numb, he had that kind of far off stare that didn't register what was happening around him and his arms were folded across his chest as if to protect himself from his surroundings. Kiran was different though, her heart was racing and she smelled like sex, all of the excitement had left her aroused, the tips of her breasts were pressed against her green shirt and her ass moved seductively in her white shorts. The blood beating throughout Hannah's body reached a crescendo, she dropped her blades and rushed forward, grabbed Kiran by the front of her waist and pulled her up close next to her. Terrified, Kiran let out a scream that echoed across the stadium; the others turned to see what was wrong, but before anyone could think or act the feral Hannah wrenched a fistful of Kiran's hair aside, exposing her neck, and with the long fangs on the top and bottom of her jaw she tore her friend's throat wide open.

Chapter 6: Aftermath

Everyone was yelling. Victory turned to pandemonium as the group of friends witnessed Hannah tear Kiran's throat out. The girl they knew was gone and in her place stood a newly born vampire with radiant marble skin that reflected the moonlight, nails as sharp as knives, fangs that could bite through steel, and black irises so large that they almost entirely blotted out the sclera. Even Hannah's black hair looked different, more electric, as if it was a dark fire being moved about by the wind. Her friend's blood dripped down her chin and neck, soaking into her already blood spattered t-shirt, and as casually as someone throwing away a used food wrapper she threw her friend's body to the ground and wiped her mouth off with the sleeve of her hoodie. Kiran landed on the ground without grace, her figure splayed out in an awkward shape on the wet grass, arms bent, legs crooked, hair tangled in leaves, and with her eyes open staring at nothing. The group remained still, in shock at what had happened, until Cassie screamed as the feral Hannah locked her deadly gaze onto her and began to move towards the rest of them.

Zeke sprang forward from the group and collided with Hannah as she was nearly upon them, tackling her and using her own momentum to knock her to the ground. Snarling and within a second she grabbed him by the collar and tossed him twenty yards on top of a car in the parking lot causing him to land on his back and to scream out in agony.

Suddenly vines and roots started to shoot out of the ground and wrap themselves around Hannah, they pulled her down and continued to weave around her until she was entirely encased in an wooden-plant cocoon.

Without anyone noticing, Merlyn had appeared next to Kiran. He straightened her contorted body out on the ground and began to move his hands over and above her while he recited a mystical prayer. **"Locitus solane ectus, locitus solane ectus, locitus solane ectus,"** he said exactly nine times. Taking a pocket knife out of his jeans he flicked it open and slashed his left palm, held it over Kiran and let the blood drop into the wounds in her neck. After a minute of silence

Kiran's eyes blinked and she gasped as she sat up and then fell back down again, the injuries to her throat had started to close, leaving behind a fresh scar.

"You two!" He shouted pointing to Cassie and Matt. "Go grab the football player, I'm getting us the hell out of here right now." The kids stood there frozen. "Go!" Jarred from their shock they took off as fast as they could to the parking lot and Zeke. Merlyn tried to focus his attention on Kiran once more but was distracted by the sound of something being ripped apart. Hannah burst through the cocoon that had been holding her and charged at him, she crossed twenty yards in a flash, leapt into the air and came down with her arms outstretched, ready to tear his head off. **"BLASTAAR!"** He shouted. A blue spike of energy shaped like a ram shot out of one of the bone wands and hit

Hannah the entire length of her body. The impact knocked her back to the football field and out cold. Breathing heavy from the effort Merlyn remained kneeling by Kiran, his left arm outstretched holding one of the Bonham drumsticks, shaking.

Cassie and Matt returned with Zeke, they were both helping to support him although he'd walked back on his own. "We're back," said Cassie. "What next?"

"Stay here with Kiran, I'm going to get Hannah." Cassie and Matt watched him walk over to the football field and pick her up, he carried her back in his arms at a slow pace, staggering here and there, clearly winded and tired as hell. Matt left Cassie and Zeke and ran over to help.

"Here," he said as he put his arms under Hannah on either side of Merlyn's. "You look like you're about to fall over, man."

"Thanks," said Merlyn. "But if she wakes up I want you to run the hell away. Got it?"

"Run for my life. Roger that."

They set Hannah's body down a few feet from Kiran and backed away, Merlyn kept himself between the two while Matt went over to stand next to Cassie and Zeke, who was leaning against her and holding his side. "All right, everyone get as close as you can, I'm going to Star Trek our asses up to the observatory before something else stupid happens."

"We're going to freaking teleport?" Asked Zeke.

"Damn right we are. Everyone hold onto your cookies." Merlyn grabbed his drumsticks out of his back pocket, raised his arms to the sky and spoke the magic words. **"Cho E'chu."**

"Wait a second," said Zeke. "Did you just say that in Klingon?"

Merlyn grinned as hundreds tiny spots in the air began to sparkle like gold coins falling from the sky, they drifted down onto the group increasing in size and brightness, and as everyone began to feel a tingling throughout their bodies there was a sudden flash and they were gone.

*****

The observatory appeared around everyone spinning like a carnival ride, the giant telescope and thousand of arcane artifacts, slowing little by little until everything was still at last. Matt and Zeke were sick to their stomachs, and lost their lunches on the concrete floor.

"Sorry 'bout that," said Merlyn. "First time teleporting's a real bitch for some people."

Zeke looked at Cassie. "You're not sick?" He asked.

"Nope." Cassie patted her belly and smiled. "Stomach like a superhero."

"Jesus," said Matt. "Best fricken' power ever right now. Blargh."

"Double blargh," said Zeke.

Merlyn bent down to check on Kiran and then Hannah. "Matt, I need you to help me get Hannah to the other side of the observatory. You two, please take Kiran and set her down on the bed in the room on the other side of the living room." He pointed to Cassie and Zeke, then gestured through the adjoining doorway, which lead to the living room, kitchen, stairs and hallway on the opposite side; down the hallway both upstairs and downstairs there were a dozen more rooms, several of which had been turned into bedrooms.

Matt opened the door to the far bedroom and was taken aback by what he saw, it was a large but Spartan room with a small bed in one corner with a chair and nightstand next to it, and a large cross with a circle around it in the middle of the concrete floor. In the center of the circle were two pairs of heavy iron manacles attached to the floor with steel chains, they sat Hannah down inside of it, Merlyn went over to the nightstand, opened the top drawer, grabbed a pair of thick gloves, a key, and an old beaten up Catholic bible with a dark brown cover and lots of sticky notes marking passages. He put the gloves on, unlocked the manacles and started fastening them to Hannah's wrists and ankles, when he was finished he stepped outside of the circle, removed the pair of gloves and waved his right hand in front of his chest with the palm out, making the kind of sweeping motion you'd make if you were cleaning a piece of glass. A bright blue flame erupted from the line of the circle, rose up from the floor to the ceiling and then disappeared. "Protection circle, she's inside of a sort of mystical cage right now," he said to Matt. "It's a scary scene but it needs to be done, she has to be secure before I can get control of the vamp inside of her."

"Yeah, I kinda figured that it wasn't going to be easy. She'll be okay though, won't she?" Said Matt.

"I hope so," said Merlyn. "I think so, I'll do everything I can. A lot of what happens next will be up to Hannah. Come on, I need to check on your other friend and get her squared away before the really fun job begins."

"Don't worry about that, she'll beat it." Said Matt.

Merlyn checked on Kiran for a minute and then left Matt with her and the others, he walked out to an ice chest sitting beside an astronaut's empty space suit in the observatory, dug through a top layer of beer bottles and steaks, then retrieved a bottle of blood and a bottle of plasma from the bottom of it. Back in the bedroom with Kiran and the others he hooked her up to receive a transfer of both. "She should be okay in a few hours, I healed the wounds to her body before but she was desperately low on blood after Hannah attacked her. The transfusion will finish the expedited healing process."

"Whose blood is that?" Asked Cassie.

"Mine," said Merlyn. "Wizard blood is universal, it can also regenerate almost any wound."

"That go for you too?" Asked Matt. "Just how old are you anyway?"

"Old." Replied Merlyn.

"Holy crap! You're like the Doctor." Exclaimed Cassie.

"Nah, I bet he's more like Wolverine." Said Zeke.

"I'm far less hairy," said Merlyn. "Watch over your friend, there's food in the kitchen if you get hungry, and showers upstairs if you want to clean up. I'm going to try to help Hannah. This may take hours, whatever you do, whatever you hear, do not enter that room." Five minutes later the solid steel door to the far bedroom was locked and the others were gathered in the hallway listening to the screaming inside.

*****

The vampire inside of Hannah had a firm hold on her and wouldn't let go without a fight, the struggle between the creature and Merlyn's attempts to banish it to the recesses of Hannah's supernatural id were akin to the most dangerous of exorcisms. Her screams and shouts carried throughout the whole building, little of the person remained, only the beast. Standing outside of the protection circle Merlyn held open an old Catholic Bible and recited prayer after prayer in Latin, all the while splashing the creature in Hannah's body with holy water. Taking his eyes off of the book for a moment he glanced inside of the circle. "I know you're in there," he said. "Help me collar this damn thing, Hannah."

Thunder crashed above the observatory, shaking the walls, the roof and the foundation; the force of it moved the bed from its far corner in the room right into the circle, breaking the protective barrier, feral Hannah reacted without hesitation. Merlyn hadn't taken into account that her natural super human strength had increased exponentially as a vampire, she ripped the chains out of the floor, crossed the room in blinding speed, and slashed open his stomach in one stroke with her razor sharp claws. As the wizard fell backwards he dropped everything and covered his abdomen with his hands to prevent his insides from falling out, for a moment his hands glowed red and then they burned

white hot as he sealed the fatal wound. Reeling from the colossal effort it took to heal himself, Merlyn became enraged, his eyes turned red and they sparked as if a welder's torch had touched a metal surface, the chains on the floor rose into the air, wrapping themselves around Hannah from head to toe, and tightening both fists he summoned a telekinetic gale that slammed Hannah into the brick wall, pushing the outline of her body several inches deep.

Snatching a wooden cross off of the nightstand Merlyn rushed over to the immobilized vampire and held it against her forehead, her skin started to cook, it boiled and it blistered, smoke drifted to the ceiling and the seared flesh smelled like a fat greasy piece of bacon frying in a skillet. "I don't want to do this but I have to," said Merlyn. "Please forgive me." He let the cross fall to the floor and in his two hands he conjured red-yellow flames, a moment passed as they grew larger and hotter, engulfing his forearms, and then he did the unspeakable, he set Hannah Harrison's whole body on fire.

Her screams were deafening, both the beast and the girl were in agony, their suffering was palpable through the whole of the observatory to everyone inside it's walls. Merlyn picked the cross up from the ground and again placed it next to Hannah's face inside of the fire, it seared her flesh to the bone; acrid smoke rose from her burning body to the ceiling, her charred clothes crumbled to ash onto the concrete floor, and the remainder of her skin reddened to a scorched crimson hue under the heat of the fire. An eerie darkness spread over the room, pitch black but for the light of the flames consuming Hannah's body, the wizard, be it a trick of the shadows or a spell appeared to grow ten feet tall. Towering above her, he shouted, **"GET THE HELL OUT!"**

A spectre tore itself free from Hannah's body and struck at the wizard, it was demonic in form but without substance, shaped as a human but distorted; with harsh angular lines, misshapen skull, large claws and the jagged fangs of prehistoric predators. Like a wisp of mist the ghost vamp dissipated as soon as it was outside of her, right away Merlyn waved his hand over the fire and it vanished, as if a giant had blown out a match, he gestured again and the chains unwrapped themselves then flew to the corner of the room. Hannah collapsed unconscious into his arms; naked, blistering and red from the flames; whatever inherited curse remained within the girl was buried deep inside of her for now. As he placed her in the bed and covered her up, the wizard noted that her burns were mending at a far quicker rate than he'd expected, *thank the Gods for superpeople and their healing factors.* The fire had been mystical not physical, designed to cleanse the spirit but not to cause long lasting harm to the body. *The cost is in pain,* thought Merlyn, *that's what's difficult to fix afterwards.*

Chapter 7: Wizardsplaining

Merlyn quietly sat down in the chair next to Hannah, she was sleeping but it was fitful; she tossed, she turned, and she muttered aloud, the nightmares evident in her expressions, at times yelling so loud that her friends would stop by to see if everything was okay. They'd look and linger, concerned that something awful was going to happen, even Kiran, now awake and feeling much better would come by to sit next to her and hold her hand for a while. The wizard explained that she was going to be fine but that vampiric episodes were like an infection, they took a while to recover from. After a while he'd kick them out and sit down again, he was beyond worn out, *Hannah isn't the only one that needs time to recover.* It was the hour of the wolf, between 3 and 4 in the morning, that terrible time when you're exhausted and want to sleep but can't; in the past several hours he had used more magicks than some do in a lifetime, it would take hours, possibly days before he was at full strength again. Merlyn's eyes grew heavy, sleep seemed like a luxury but perhaps a necessary one, his head dipped to his chest and he dozed off in the chair, but he didn't dream, there was no time for such things this night.

An unbearable heat surged throughout Hannah's body as she woke up, she was soaked in sweat, her throat was raw and her eyes were blurry. Her head pounded and she was confused, nothing made sense except a deep primal need somewhere inside of her. She saw Merlyn leaning back in a chair next to the bed with his eyes closed, breathing softly; he smelled like sweat too, and apples. Someone had removed all of her clothes except for her t-shirt and underwear before placing her in the bed; as she crawled out and set foot upon the floor she moved her hand down to feel how wet she was, the blood in her veins pounded inside of her, a flood of desire behind a wall of conscience shouting for release. Hannah climbed on top of the wizard and as his eyes opened she kissed him with a reckless fervor, she moved her hips back and forth feeling him stiffen beneath her, and then reaching down to undo his pants a bolt of painful ice cold misery went through every inch of her, it

was so jarring that she stumbled back, tripped over the bed and landed on her butt right in the middle of concrete floor.

"Frigidum," she heard Merlyn gasp.

"Ouch!" Exclaimed Hannah as she grimaced and rubbed her bum. "Um, where are my pants?"

"Here," said Merlyn as he tossed Hannah her pants form the back of the chair. He turned around to give her some privacy. "For the record, I was not the one who dressed you in new clothes, your fiend Cassie did that. I asked her to go to your house and to get you something to wear."

"What…uh, happened to what I was wearing?"

"They all burned off when I set you on fire."

"Wonderful…wait a second, so you saw me naked? And why the hell did you set me on fire?" Asked Hannah in an angry and shocked tone.

"Yes, as the day you were born," said Merlyn. "Regarding your second question, how much about what happened after the zombie fight at school do you remember?"

"Oh my God," she gasped. "I remember all of it, it's like something I saw on television but I still know what I did." Hannah wrapped her arms around her knees on the floor and started to cry. "Is Kiran dead?"

"No. I got to her in time, she's been healing all night, physically she should be fine by now. She and the others have been coming in all night long to see how you are."

Hannah bounded up from the floor and hugged Merlyn so hard that she felt his back pop. "Thank you, thank you, thank you."

"It's all right," he said, "Everything's going to be all right."

Taking her arms away from Merlyn she moved to the bed and sat back down. "Can't believe how horrible last night was, but it did answer a few things for me. I guess my dad was a vampire, huh?" Said Hannah. "Funny how my mom forgot to mention that part when she would talk about him. Some hero. You must have known too."

"I did, it's one of the reasons I gave you the swords, I thought the enchantments might temper the vampirism. I'm so sorry that I was wrong." He leaned forward. "Don't sell your dad short, David Walker was one of the bravest men I've ever met. He fought the curse and the hunger for longer than any vampire I've ever met, and he sacrificed himself to save the world. Your mom too, she let go of the only person she's ever loved for the greater good."

"I suppose she just couldn't talk about it," said Hannah. "Some warning would've been nice though. Super powers from her and a supernatural bloodlust from him, that's just awesome. So what do I do now? Am I going to Hulk out every time things get crazy?"

"I don't think so, this happened because it was inevitable, it's who you are. Vampirism is like a Mystical STD that's passed along in the blood. New vampires are sired by being fed on and then by feeding on the vamp that attacked them right before the moment of death, for a full on vampire the thirst is irresistible, it's the thing that drives them. In your case, you're a superhuman/vampire hybrid, I don't believe there has ever been a being like you before. In your case a vampire outbreak is a little more like herpes, problematic but treatable. The magical Linda Blair cleanse that you just went through should keep you from vamping out for a good long time. Big risk now is that you've had a taste of human blood you may want more, the hunger is seductive, most vampires start out not wanting to become monsters but that's what they end up as anyway, they can't help it, like the scorpion stinging the frog, it's their nature. Be mindful."

"Oh my God, that was a uncomfortable analogy. Could you explain that to me again but in a way that doesn't use the phrase 'Mystical STD'? Thanks."

"Yeah, on second thought that was really awful," said Merlyn. "Okay, you're a supernatural hybrid with near unlimited power, don't Hulk out and do horrible evil shit."

"Are there other hybrids?" Asked Hannah. "Other children made the old fashioned hot and sweaty way."

"Some, thing is, they aren't immortal like regular vamps, so they die out over time, and the Bela Lugosi types don't like 'em so they usually try to kill each other whenever they come into contact. It's an animal thing, they do it to protect their place at the top of the food chain.
Hybrids are stronger and have fewer weaknesses, that makes them a threat to the vampires and their children, the sired."

"I thought vampires couldn't have kids, what with being dead and soulless."

"First, forget that soul nonsense, no such thing." Said Merlyn. "We're all basically made up of mass and energy, vampires are no different, that mass, that energy just changes over time, but when they're sired they're basically still the same person they were before, it's the hunger that changes them. Hard to think of humanity in a positive light when they're your food."

"And the kids?"

"Here goes. Two vampires can't have children, they're both dead. A female can't have a child because her body is no longer a vessel that can support life. But on rare occasions a male vampire will still produce sperm and can have a child with a human woman, think about it, no matter how old males get we can still have kids. Hybrids are a special kind of badass, all of the powers of the vampire except the immortality and none of the weaknesses; sunlight doesn't bother them, they like crosses, they can eat as much garlic as they want, they're invulnerable to fire, silver is no problem, and they are much much stronger. Like Silver Age Superman compared to Golden Age Superman strong." Merlyn paused. "And you make all of them look weak."

"So why did I turn into a mindless rage monster when I vamped out?" Asked Hannah.

"That's what happens at first, most hybrids are human until that day when they vamp out, and it's like that for a while, it's another reason why the thirst is so unbeatable. As they change more and more their personality starts to assert itself through the rage and they usually stay in their vampire form longer until that's all that they are."

"Sounds like a bunch of inevitable awfulness," said Hannah. "Screw that."

"Exactly, I don't think it has to be that way with you. You can fight it. Your other side, the part of you that wants to protect people is way stronger."

"Good, then that's the way that it's going to be, you say what you did helped and that the swords will help. Well from now on I know what I need to prevent, I won't let it happen again."

"I was hoping that would be your attitude, now there's another thing." Merlyn pulled his chair up closer to the bed and leaned forward, "I need to tell you something."

"Oh god, that's never good," said Hannah. "What the hell is it now? Did my favorite show get canceled? Oh wait, I'm mystically pregnant aren't I. The devil's spawn is going to erupt from my belly in six days like that creepy ass thing from the Alien movies."

"You mean the xenomorph?" Asked Merlyn.

"Yes."

"No, you're not going to have the devil's alien love child," said Merlyn. "Yet. That's not scheduled to happen for another couple of years."

"What? The fuck."

"Kidding."

"Clever. I don't think Doc Frankenstein's the only asshole wizard in town this week."

"Enough jokes." Merlyn stopped, looked away to collect his thoughts and then looked back at Hannah again. "Your friend was dead."

She stared at him in disbelief. "What's that supposed to mean?"

"It means," he said, "that I cannot cheat death, I can only prolong life. Death will come for her, be it five years from now or ten, the reaper will come. And you can count on it being sooner rather than later."

"I don't buy it," said Hannah. "People like us, like my mom, we cheat death all of the time. There has to be a way."

"There probably is but I don't know it, at least not yet, I will keep looking though, I promise."

"So that's it, maybe I didn't do it today, but I killed my best friend. Jesus Christ, how do I live with that?"

"I wish I could say that it was going to get easier for you but it won't," said Merlyn. "Your life will be full of burdens, this is only the first."

"Well, that helps." Said Hannah. "Kinda. Sorta. Not really." Her features grew somber and she looked away, it was several minutes before she spoke again. "Does Kiran know?"

"Yeah, I told her right away, figured she needed to know immediately with all of the craziness going on."

"Good. I need to see her, please."

"Of course."

*****

Merlyn left Hannah with Kiran while he attempted to help Matt. He found him asleep on the couch in the living room, snoring, very loud, he tapped him on the shoulder until he woke up. "Hey, kid, wake up. Me Yoda, you Skywalker, time for a lesson."

"But I don't want to go to school today, mom," said Matt. "There's a cranky ass wizard there who wants to show me his wand."

"Hilarious," said Merlyn. "Meet me outside by the big oak tree in front of the building."

Merlyn sat beneath the big oak tree with his legs crossed and his back to the trunk, about five minutes of irritating waiting passed until Matt joined him, the kid's shoes were untied, he was stifling a yawn and he was eating from a bag of the wizard's Cheetos, his last bag. *If I kill him the girls will be mad, maybe a light maiming,* he thought. "Sit down."

It was just before dawn, the grass was still wet and the eastern sun was only now beginning to peak over the horizon, casting its light on the plains. Matt sat down a few feet from the wizard and shifted himself around a bit trying to get comfortable. "It's really pretty out here," he said. "It's sad how little I usually notice things like that."

"This is a good time for us to talk, the world is waking up, the day is new and full of possibilities, much like yourself."

"I don't know about that," said Matt. "Mostly I feel like a screw up these days."

"Trust me, that's about the most normal thing you could ever say, we all feel that way from time to time."

"Even badass wizards?" Asked Matt.

"Especially badass wizards," said Merlyn. "I have a lifetime of mistakes to make up for already, and a couple of future ones that seem inevitable at this point. There are things in my life that I have no choice about."

"That's comforting. I guess." Said Matt.

"But you on the other hand are at a crossroads, you have a choice to make, and it will determine the rest of your life. The majeesh opened the door to the Witchery Way for you, but now it's up to you to take that first step into a larger existence all by yourself."

"What do I do?" Asked Matt.

"You have to reach out with your mind," said Merlyn. "In order to not be controlled by the darkness you have to be bigger than it is. And luckily that's kind of easy, reality by its nature is just very very large, you have to embrace that."

"So I need to become one with the God damn force?" Asked Matt.

"Yeah, pretty much, just remember that it's all connected," said Merlyn. "And that you are a piece of that bigger reality, not apart, not better, but one of."

"Um, cool. I think I can do that. Kinda. Maybe. I really don't understand what the hell you're talking about. It sounds like new age bullshit."

"Okay, valid point, but keep this in mind," said Merlyn. "You can be whoever and whatever you want, literally and figuratively. You have that power and it is a breathtaking and beautiful thing, but if you let outside forces control you, dictate to you, then they will destroy you. Without a doubt that is what will happen. So be careful and be on guard. The world's a scary place."

"And how do I stop that? Like literally, what the eff do I do?"

"Be vigilant. Practice. Simply sit and think. Reach out with your thoughts to the world around you. If you do that, you really will figure it out."

"Okay," said Matt.

"And go track down a shaman who can teach you about these things, I'm making this shit up as I go along."

"Son of a bitch," exclaimed Matt with a deep belly laugh.

"Here endeth the lesson," said Merlyn standing up. "Now go gather up everyone and bring them to the living room, we have serious business to discuss."

*****

Hannah padded into Kiran's room wearing the Tauntaun slippers Cassie had brought her from home, they made a soft thumping noise as her feet hit the concrete floor. "Guess you heard."

"Yeah," Kiran replied.

"I am so so very sorry, whatever it takes, I will fix this. The whole world's full of crazy magic and solutions to problems we've never even heard of, there has to be something out there that can keep you alive."

"I know." Kiran was adamant in her tone as she stared at Hannah and then jumped out of bed to give her a big bear hug.

"Um...you know? What?" Asked Hannah as she squeezed her best friend back.

"I mean, I know we'll fix things and we'll kick the Grim Reaper's ass before he gets me." She said. "I've lived my entire life in this bizarro town, seen things that would scare most people's poop white, watched you thump baddies who you never should have been able to defeat, and we always win. So sure, I'm frightened, but I know without question that we'll figure it out before my battery runs dry."

"You're not mad?"

"Livid….turns out Merle's wizard blood packs more happy bang that Tylenol 3 though, it's a little difficult to be mad at anything right now."
She gave Hannah a brief smile. "Except the ending of Lost, that still sucked. Hard."

"Right!?" Said Hannah. "Six seasons of awesomeness and then it all comes down to them being dead maybe and getting to wake up in some parallel reality waiting room."

"And don't forget the blinky buried island lights," said Kiran. "Stupid machine looked like it was lit up by the thing in the briefcase from Pulp Fiction. I still say the island was an alien spaceship."

"Oh sweety," said Hannah. "That's just dumb, it wasn't a spaceship."

Pfffttt. "Totally a spaceship, was probably sent to pick up the Heaven's Gate loons and got, wait for it. Lost."

"Ugh, I hate you so much right now."

"You love me and you know it, I'm deliciously bitable even," said Kiran. "So, I guess you're a big bad she-vampire, huh?"

"Yup," said Hannah. She hesitated and grinned at Kiran, the overwhelming sense of guilt evident on her face. It took a few seconds until she was able to say something. "We're just going by vampires these days though, there was a whole thing about equal undead rights back in the seventies." *When in doubt make a dumb joke,* she thought.

"I take it your mom never really filled you in about your dad, huh?"

"Thought she had, she told me tons of things about him, apparently she skipped over the big vampire stuff."

"Well that's a hell of a surprise," said Kiran.

"For all of us," said Hannah. "I am so so sorry, Kiran. Whatever it takes, I promise that I'll fix this."

"It's really okay, not lying, not in shock anymore, I know you will. You're a heroic do-gooder badass, it's not even a question."

Hannah jumped on the bed and gave Kiran a huge back breaking hug. "I ever tell you how much I love the shit out of you?"

"Nowhere near enough," replied Kiran as she squeezed back.

"Wow," said Matt as he leered inside the doorway. "It's a shame I'm not straight right now."

"Right?!" Exclaimed Hannah. "We could totally NC-17 this scene."

"Promises promises," said Matt. "Some best friends, you two should totally find me a nice fella."

"We're working on it," said Kiran. "I mean, geez, we only had one day of school this year before the evil douche mojo struck."

"Stupid evil." Said Matt. "Okay, time to put your pants on, teen Gandalf wants to talk to us."

*****

The league of monster fighting friends gathered together in the living room next to the observatory, Cassie and Zeke sat close to each other on the lumpy and comfortable couch, Kiran and Matt sat across from one another at the dinner table, meanwhile Merlyn paced back and forth muttering to himself and Hannah remained in the little kitchen alcove brewing coffee in an old stainless steel percolator while she hummed the Pixies *Where Is My Mind* to herself.

"But why does all of the crazy bullshit happen here?" Asked Kiran in an exasperated voice.

Hannah poked her head out of the kitchen. "You want to field this one, wizard boy? I know how much you love exposition." She asked.

"Gods yes," said an excited Merlyn. "Alright, does anyone know what a Ley Line is?"

"Yeah," squeaked Cassie. "It's like a magical fault line in the Earth, weird stuff happens around them."

"That's exactly right, they're cracks between our dimension and the ones that we're neighbors with, sometimes things slip through those cracks and sometimes they act like giant mystical crazy magnets, pulling all sorts of supernatural things to them. Now these Ley Lines run all over the world and every once in a while they meet, when they do we call that a crossroads or a convergence, and in those places the weirdness really steps it up a notch, crossroads amplify the magicks and strangeness of places and people, and the walls between the dimensions become very weakened. These are the kinds of locations where you'll usually find your big players in the supernatural game."

Hannah brought out cups for everyone and poured coffee, it was almost morning and they all seemed to perk up from their exhaustion once they started to sip the dark ambrosia. She grabbed one for herself, poured in an aged and cherished mug with tiny spider web cracks throughout, adorned with black serif sans writing that said "The Boss," and then sat down in a comfy brown leather chair next to the couch with a high back. *Wish I had a villainous pussy to stroke right now,* she thought. *Jesus Christ, Hannah, it's Armageddon, I almost ate my best friend, and I still can't pass up a horrible double entendre. Thank god no one can hear me think.* She looked over at Matt who had a sneaky all to knowing grin on his face. *Damn it.*

"So Serenity's a convergence then," said Kiran. "That's why we get all of the crazy nonsense happening around here."

"No," said Merlyn. "Serenity isn't just any convergence, it's THE Convergence, think King Kong in comparison to Mighty Joe Young." Everybody stared blankly at him. "Okay, no pop culture love on that one. Imagine a really big monkey compared to an even bigger skyscraper sized monkey. In the entire world there are maybe only two or three other places like this."

"More than two Ley Lines come together here, don't they?" Asked Matt.

"A lot more," said Merlyn.

"How many?" Asked Kiran.

"Five," said Merlyn. "And that's the most you can have, at least that's what most mystical scholars say, nobody's ever witnessed six. Imagine a pentagram, now from each point of the star draw a line to the middle, where they meet in the center is where Serenity is located."

"The convergence of convergences, right smack in the center of a giant pentagram located in the middle of the heartland in the good ol' U. S. of A." Said Hannah. "Some fun, huh, guys? That's what we're up against here when we fight."

"Did you know about all of this?" Asked Zeke.

"Most of it, my mom would fill me in bit by bit over the years, I never realized the scope of it until right now."

"How do we win then?" Said Kiran. "Can we even beat Doc Frankenstein and his zombies and his snake guy and his big Kirby machine o' evil?"

"Hell yeah we can win, mom's been beating the bad guys since she was our age. Right now she's beneath the city confronting the enemy and figuring out what to do. For now we sit back and wait to hear from her, then we back whatever her play is. In this fight she's the superhero and we're all the sidekicks."

The group collectively paused after listening to Hannah's speech, and to all outward appearances seemed to relax. Matt told Kiran a joke that received a hanging motion with a stuck out tongue, Cassie and Zeke snuggled on the couch while whispering and giggling to each other, and Hannah closed her eyes for a moment, simply smelling her coffee. *Peace of mind exists between those moments you cannot control,* she thought.

Merlyn ducked into the observatory and went over to a work bench near the telescope, a handful of old metal coins, gray-green and with faded writing lay scattered in the upper right corner near a reading lamp, he grabbed two of them, shoved them into his pocket, and then returned to the living room.

"Alright," said Merlyn in a loud voice as he clapped his hands together and pointed to Hannah. "Looks like we're all up to speed, you and I have a road trip ahead of us."

"What?" Said Hannah.

"You need answers to questions you don't know you even have yet, and I know just the place."

"Shouldn't we stick around and y'know, get ready to fight the bad guys."

"Nonsense, we'll be travelling to another dimension, time works different there, we'll be back before you know it. Maybe a day or two there but only a couple of hours here." Merlyn pulled the coin out of his pocket and twirled it between his fingers. "Oh, and grab the swords, you might need them. They're in the observatory over next to the guillotine, I found a cool criss-cross back scabbard thing and stuffed them in there."

"You're completely insane," said Hannah as she set down her coffee and went to get the Celestial Twins.

"Noted," he said. "The rest of you get some rest, we'll be back soon."

Hannah returned to the living room and slipped the swords onto her back. "Okay, guys, just chill out and rest up for a few hours, you'll need it." Everyone grinned at the identical instructions from both of their would be leaders. "You're the driver, wizard boy, let's get going."

Merlyn flipped the coin onto the floor, as it landed it began to spin faster and faster until a cone shaped vortex erupted from it, full of light and shadows, people and buildings, images human and too alien for anyone to understand. The wizard spoke a loud incantation in a long forgotten language and the pictures inside of the light settled down to one, a beautiful golden wheat field that stretched as far as the eye could see.

"So what do we do now?" Asked Hannah.

"We jump," said Merlyn. He held out his hand and smiled towards Hannah, a mischievous look in his eyes.

"You are a rascal and a charmer, Mr. Merlyn. Let us away!" She took his hand in hers and they both bunny rabbit hopped into the vortex; the lights swirled for a moment and then disappeared, the coin stopped spinning, and as everyone watched, Merlyn and Hannah were gone. The rest of the group let out a sigh at seeing them disappear, like the air had been released from a balloon.

"Wow," said Matt. "It's one thing to teleport, it's another to actually see it."

"Yeah, it's way better, less barfy feelings," said Zeke. "All in all I'll stick with being the McCoy of the crew, no teleporting for me."

"What a bunch of baby men," said Cassie. "I didn't feel a thing. Course, women are much tougher than men."

"Hell yeah," said Kiran as she came over and high fived Cassie.

"What're you bragging about? You were passed out vamp food when we came got here." Said Matt.

"Aw, you boys are just jealous of our sisterly bond," said Kiran.

As they laughed the world fell apart around them, the whole building shook, furniture moved, dishes crashed off of tables and cupboards, knickknacks careened from one side of the room to the other, and several large cracks split down the concrete floor and the brick walls. Everyone hustled to a doorway until the shaking stopped, but it wasn't a single tremor that they felt, instead it was a series of them that lasted for over two minutes. After they were certain the quake was over the group ran outside, looking down on Serenity from the hilltop they all witnessed a disaster unlike anything any of them had ever seen. Fires dotted the town from one end to the other, smoke drifted heavily in the a.m. sky, sirens blared, alarms wailed, the lights were off in at least a third of the city, and as the dust cleared over the skyline it was obvious that three or four tall buildings downtown had collapsed. Stunned, the four of them just stared, Cassie began to tremble and cry, at last looking away and sobbing into Zeke's chest as he held her. Kiran and Matt put their arms around one another as well, each supporting the other, unless they might fall over from shock.

Kiran broke their silence, "Mother. Fucker. Someone is going to pay for this."

"Jesus H. Christ, hurry back soon, Hannah." Said Matt. "If we ever needed our superhero, it's right now."

Chapter 8: The Battle Below

The Valkyrie's armor shined in the moonlight as she walked down the street next to the dapper young soldier in his WW2 army dress uniform. Her golden hair floated in the breeze, a stark contrast to the black wings that grew from her back, so large that while folded the bottom most feathers touched the ground as she walked. She had no helm; nor sword, nor spear, nor shield, this night the soldier was all of those things to her and so she held his hand.

He looked at her and recalled the first time he had seen his beautiful Valkyrie as he lay dying in the snow, surrounded by the forest of the Ardennes. The Germans had advanced like ghosts that night, silent but for the crunch of the snow beneath their boots. His platoon had come under attack as most of them slept in their fresh dug bunkers in the near frozen round, no warning was given, the Germans had slipped in and killed the forward sentries without making a sound. A chorus of murder and death had awoken him that night as he listened to his brothers final
creams, for a man so cold and whose hands were numb he'd been quick to grab his rifle and bayonet.

The first German he killed that night appeared over his bunker looking in, he fired a single shot that entered through the bottom of his jaw and exited through the top of his helmet, his body tumbled forward into the pit, almost landing on top of him. Climbing out he encountered the second German who fired a shot and somehow missed him, knocking his rifle aside with his own he stabbed the man in the belly several times and tossed him back into the hole in the ground. By that time several of the enemy had heard the commotion and were headed towards him firing their weapons, he was shot twice in the left arm, once in the right leg, and still managed to pick off two more of them, as he fell to the ground he saw a German the size of a small tank come through the trees, but no matter how many times he shot him the behemoth wound not fall. As he wavered on his knees in the snow, out of ammunition, the big man approached, leveled his luger pistol at him and said, "Gut Gekampft, Krieger." As the bullet entered his chest he remembered thinking, *I wonder what it means.*

He laid there in the cold for what seemed like an eternity with his blood pouring out onto the snow; delusional, feverish, warm at last, and dying. It was so dark that night that he couldn't see, until the light came towards him through the fog and the trees; it was a woman, with golden hair and silver armor, riding a white horse with a black leather saddle. His Valkyrie. She wore a sword in a scabbard on her left side, an iron shield on her back, and she clutched a five foot long spear in her right hand. Stopping several feet away she dismounted from her horse and walked over to him, her feet though wrapped in high leather boots barely left an impression in the snow, she laid her spear down next to him and bent down to feel his forehead, her hand felt warm. Lightly her hair brushed his bloody face and her smile looked like an angel's, "It will be all right," she whispered.

Taking a deep breath the soldier closed his eyes and felt himself leave the forest, two weeks later he woke up in a hospital a few miles outside of London to the face of an angel.

It didn't make any sense to him at the time but somehow his beautiful Valkyrie turned out to be the nurse that was taking care of him in the hospital, most people would question whether or not what they saw was real, yet when he looked at her he knew without doubt or hesitation that what he had seen in the forest had not been a dream. She healed him, and over the next several weeks as they talked and held hands and stole quick kisses they fell into a deep love. And for the next thirty three years that followed they were inseparable; through happiness, adventure, and strife, they never left each other's side. Not until the blackout in New York City during the Summer of '77.

To be with her now in Serenity was bittersweet, a spectre and a goddess reunited after so long apart, a solemn task ahead for them to complete. They stood in front of the Harrison home and watched as Sarah moved about.

"You cannot help her," she said, "and neither can I."

"I know," said the soldier.

The Valkyrie took the soldiers face in her hands and gently kissed him on the lips, "But we can at least watch over her and keep her soul safe from harm."

"It feels like so little," he said.

"No," replied the Valkyrie. "It is everything."

They stayed there for a long time holding one another, watching as their daughter armed herself to fight another war against the darkness. Pride and sorrow swelled inside their hearts as they looked on their lost child, helpless but to bear witness to the unfolding events ahead of her.

*****

The old wooden box was about the size of an old army footlocker, it was sanded smooth and stained a dark robust red, ornate carvings of scenes from Norse Mythology adorned the rounded top and the body, as well as dozens of runes that were etched into the border and joint pieces. There was no lock, and there was no latch, Sarah knelt in front of it and whispered the incantation Merlyn had given her so many years before, **"Arctis Avengus."** Slowly the lid opened in front of her, its ancient metal hinges were silent, revealing inside of the chest a four foot long ancient Antlantean warhammer. It lay on a bed of pure white feathers, gray metal, adorned with gold and silver, shining as bright as the day it was created, wrought with enchanted steel and forged by the greatest alchemist-blacksmith of forgotten Atlantis. Or so Merlyn had told her, he said that it had had thousands of names over the millennia but that the Vikings had called it Feigr-enda, The Doombringer. And like Thor's hammer, Mjolnir, only the worthy could possess it, but in this case, those worthy few capable of inflicting bloodshed and death.

113

Sarah lifted the warhammer from it's bed, grabbed a duffel bag full of sharp weapons by the front door and set off in her car for the private airport south of Serenity, nestled among the fields and the farms of Toth County where her friend would be arriving soon. As she left the city and passed into the country she checked the time on the dashboard, only about thirty minutes until the monster said that he would be landing in the church's plane, plenty of time to get there first. Throughout the entire summer evening drive the beauty of her surroundings were interrupted by flashes of violence, she didn't think about vampires often, not since she and the others had gotten rid of them almost twenty years ago, but for some reason at this moment she couldn't stop thinking about them. *I should be with my daughter,* she thought, *something's happened, I can feel it. Damn you, Merlyn, if you don't take care of her I'll kill you myself when all of this is over.*

After driving for almost half an hour Sarah turned the Waggoneer down an unmarked dirt road that wound through more green and gold fields, and around several lush small hills covered in flowers and grass that sloped into a little valley. Resting in the middle of the flattened vale was a two story off white building next to a flight control tower, three modest sized airplane hangars and a long paved runway, she pulled into one of only a half dozen parking spaces outside just as she spotted a jet over the eastern horizon. She walked in and through the two story building, waved to an elderly man half sleeping behind a desk covered with papers and with his feet up, the man nodded back in recognition and then resumed his nap. As the jet touched down on the tarmac Sarah exited the building and waited for it to taxi around back to her, she put her sun glasses on to diminish the twilight glare, thrust her hands into her jean pockets and began to hum a tune; *When the Saints Go Marching In,* that ol' New Orleans Funeral Dirge that she was fond of for numerous melancholy reasons.

The sun was setting in the west, the long shadow of the hills reached deep into the valley, and a cold wind had arrived from the north, tempering the warm summer evening. After a couple of minutes the plane came to a halt some fifty feet from where Sarah stood, the door opened, but instead of a set of stairs being lowered a large figure silhouetted against the cabin light leaped into the air and landed not two yards away. Frankenstein's Monster.

"Show off." Said Sarah.

The monster of legend was always an impressive sight, Colonel Karl Hesse had been a large and impressive man serving in the Prussian Army two hundred years ago but in his death he was a towering presence of strength and courage at over seven feet tall. He wore black ops army fatigues, carried a large floral Hawaiian suitcase stuffed with firearms sticking out, and had an enormous sword and a battleaxe strapped to his back. "Ja, vhat is the point of having super strength unless you can impress beautiful women in mortal danger?"

"I've known you for over twenty years and I could swear that your English accent gets worse every time I see you. Vhat is up vith that?"

He let out a bellowing laugh. "Hello, Huntress. It is good see you again."

"Hiya, big guy." Frankenstein's Monster picked up Sarah The Huntress and gave her the biggest bear hug that she'd had in years. Laughing and with her arms pinned to her sides she said, "Okay, okay, put me down, geez, now I know how my daughter feels." They walked through the building again to the Waggoneer parked out front and threw his suitcase full of guns and other weapons in the back, Karl managed to wedge himself into the passage seat next to Sarah with his knees almost up to his head. "Nice suitcase," she said.

"Hmm…yes, that, a gift from a friend. I recently took my first vacation in…well, ever. I went to Hawaii."

"Wow, I bet that was interesting. Did you have a good time?"

"Not really, Oahu was being overrun with Tiki Demons at the time."

"So you had a working vacation."

"I suppose I did."

"I bet you loved every minute, I can't picture you sitting around on a beach, catching rays and getting bored."

"Yes, but just once I'd like the opportunity to find out."

The conversation tapered off and the drive into town was quiet for most of the way until the monster decided to speak, his voice was deep and reassuring. "We will save your daughter, Sarah, I promise you this. What I don't understand is why you're so worried about her? You've fought all sorts of fiends over the years and none of that has ever effected Hannah."

"She was never as directly involved before, I've always trained her, and I'd take her with me, but I was always there beside her. Since she turned 18 this summer and started to patrol on her own things have gotten more dangerous. At first I thought nothing of it, Serenity has been more or less safe from the big and evil for long time, the worst of the worst know better than to come here."

"Something has changed?"

"Yeah, a mystical drug called majeesh is being dealt on the streets, has been for a while now, I've just been too complacent playing mom that I didn't see the urgency of the problem until now. Someone's stirring up chaos out there and they're using a bunch of volatile chemical warlocks to do it." Sarah took a deep breath and continued. "There's another thing. Merlyn Morningstar is back in Serenity, not looking a day older than the last time he was here, and that son of a bitch only shows up when the world is about to go completely fucking nuts."

"But why is Hannah in so much danger?"

"It's one of those damned if you do, damned if you don't situations. I found out he was in town from her, she stopped one of those magic junkies from mugging a family on their way home from a movie last night. Merlyn showed up after to investigate the guy and the majeesh, but then he wanted her to meet him at the school football tonight game because he senses that something will happen. The bastard, she's charmed by him, and I can't stop her and I can barely warn her because he's probably right, he always is, even if he's only telling you half of the truth."

"What else? Despite all of that I can't believe you wouldn't still hide her away from whatever all of this is."

"You're right. I went to the observatory and threatened him to leave her alone. I even beat him up a little just to make myself feel better, and after all of that he told me that he'd visited Allie in Wichita and that she and her coven had had a vision that unless Hannah was involved in the fight that she would somehow end up dead when all of this was over." Sarah paused and let out a long breath. "Then he damn near killed me. Merlyn doesn't let anything happen unless he wants it to, he allowed me to rough him up, to get it out of my system just so he'd have an excuse to remind me how freaking powerful he is."

"Could the wizard have been lying? From what I've heard, he is a master of deception and manipulation."

"That's what I was hoping, thing is, Merlyn never really lies, he simply bends the truth into whatever shape he needs it to be," said

Sarah. "But still, I called Allison this afternoon to double check, and she said it was true, the portents she's been seeing have been very clear, Hannah has to be in this fight or else she will die."

Frankenstein's Monster closed his eyes and bent his head in contemplation for a moment, when he glanced back up at Sarah he smiled; with the car window open, her sunglasses on and her hair blowing she looked fearsome and amazing to the immortal warrior. "What is your plan, Huntress?"

"It's simple," she said. "The drugs are coming up from the buried old city and someone is stealing corpses to take back down there. We're going to go below and kill all of the bad guys before they finish whatever it is they're doing."

"Ah, grave robbers, you don't suspect…?"

"I do. There's been more or less peace in this town for almost two decades, all of the creatures and the gangsters wouldn't be getting this daring unless one of the bigger bads were already here."

"Well, I guess it's a good thing you called me then. What about Hannah, should we take her with us?"

"No, the wizard's with her and he's promised to keep her safe. No matter what I may think of him, I have to believe that he means it, he's never outright lied to any of us before. She's new at this but she's powerful, they can handle whatever gets thrown at them up here, we'll deal with whatever craziness we find beneath the city."

"Have faith, my friend, we will prevail in this."

"Afraid I'm kinda short on faith these days."

"Then I will just have to have enough for both of us then." He said.

119

"The last time Serenity was staring Armageddon in the face I lost David, the hell if I'm going to sacrifice my daughter to save it this time."

"You won't have to, we'll make sure of that," he said. "I'm sorry that I wasn't able to be here for you and the battle back then, if I could have managed it I would have been proud to stand with you against the darkness."

"Well, lucky for you," said Sarah, "that's the uber-bad thing about evildoers, there's always more to fight. So, still plenty of chances for you to help out." She paused to give her friend a mischievous smile. "Besides, from what I heard, you were plenty busy fighting the good fight yourself back then."

"Yes, The Bride had raised an army of wolf-men in Romania to fight on behalf of the king of the vampires. You ridding the world of Dracul and his kind was an enormous benefit to my crusade, I daresay, I may have lost without your timely intervention. Thank you."

"Happy to help. You've never talked about her, I thought maybe Hollywood had made her up."

"It is difficult for me, in life she was the other half of my heart, in death she became my immortal enemy. Where once a deep love bonded us, after our resurrections only a warped obsession guided us to hurt the other." He turned to look out the car window and then continued. "Her name was Lady Amelie Leon, she came from a small family of nobles that had survived The Revolution and owned an estate near Paris at the end of the eighteenth century. We met at a small theatre there that was performing Moliere's *Le Misanthrope* while I was visiting the city for the first time with my family in the Summer of 1793. The atmosphere was charged with the typical political fervor of the time but there standing in the middle of it was this beautiful young woman whose demeanor and smile were as serene as the open sky, I believe that I fell in love with her the moment I saw her.

At my urging our families had dinner that evening, and I was pleased to discover that Amelie was as delightful in conversation as she was from afar. The next day we went for a walk, one that was only meant to last for an hour around the Tuileries Gardens but that instead lasted the entire day throughout the city. Being a headstrong young man of my era I was quite moved to sudden actions by the Sturm und Drang music and literature of my own people, I proposed to her that very evening outside of the newly opened Louvre Museum.

It was somewhat of a scandal to be honest, our nations were not exactly friends during this time, but I wasn't a soldier yet, and all I cared for was how she looked at me. For fifteen years she was my loving
companion, and my dearest friend, the lord never gave us children but in retrospect I understand that this was both a mercy and a blessing. While I served faithfully in the Prussian Army I would return as often as I could to our home at the foot of the Bavarian Alps, we were as happy as anyone as has a right to be in this lifetime. And then on Sunday, the 18th of June 1815, I was killed on horseback

while fighting the forces of Napoleon Bonaparte at The Battle of Waterloo. Less than a month later I was resurrected by Victor Frankenstein in his laboratory outside of Geneva. I never saw my wife alive again."

"Using Amelie was part of the doctor's great plan to bring me to heel. Our war lasted almost two years and had taken us to every corner of the globe. Each scheme for power and glory that he attempted I foiled. Finally, years later, in 1825 after I had recovered from our confrontation in the Arctic I learned that Victor had returned to Europe. For months I tracked him across the continent, following rumors to places that existed on no map, that held evidence of his unholy experiments and his use of the darkest magicks. The search was maddening, in Amsterdam I heard tales of a doctor that defied death who had left the mainland a month earlier. At last I crossed the Channel where I found him in an estate outside London, I watched him for days as I planned on how to finish him, but on the fourth night a carriage arrived with a visitor, and to my eternal dismay I discovered that it was Amelie. For two more days I watched and realized that it wasn't really my wife, The Bride was as malicious as the doctor, she assisted him in both his experiments on the living and the dead, and was a willing participant in the dark arts. What resided in the estate with the doctor was a thing like me; dead, broken, sallow and sewn back together; and lacking of any morality whatsoever. Shocked and not sure what to do next, I broke into the estate to free those being held prisoner, set fire to the whole miserable place and left the two of them there in search of answers. You see, over the next several months I found the truth, Victor Frankenstein had murdered my wife years earlier as retribution against me for my disobedience and betrayal. Bringing her back as his servant and companion was the perfect act of justice in his warped mind.

"I'm…so very very sorry, my friend." Said Sarah.

"She was always the doctor's favorite creation," said the monster. "Obedient, beautiful, without conscience, and completely insane."

"But why was she so different?" Asked Sarah. "What changed her from the woman you knew into Mrs. Evil?"

"I believe that it is because the circumstances of your death affect your resurrection. Where I died in battle fighting for a cause I believed in, Amelie was murdered in cold blood and hacked to pieces by a madman without ever knowing why. I can't imagine how scared and confused she must have been. Also, from what I've observed, following my creation, the doctor changed his spells to limit the amount of free will his subjects have. In a way their personalities are much more of an extension of his own thoughts than I ever was. A small blessing to my own cursed existence, but an important one, for over two hundred years, in my heart and my mind, I have remained myself."

"Do you know where she is now?" Said Sarah.

"At peace, I hope," said The Monster. "Following your destruction of the vampires, my allies and I were able to defeat the wolf-men and storm Dracul's fortress in pursuit of

The Bride, a dozen Swiss Guard sacrificed themselves to stop her retreat while I managed to shoot her through the heart and the head."

"Dear God."

"I dismantled her body and burned the pieces myself atop a funeral pyre blessed by the Archbishop of Bucharest, then spread her ashes among the countryside of Bavaria where we had been happy for so long."

Twilight had become night while the old soldier told his tale, stars canvassed the clear sky and the waxing moon illuminated the land. "If he's there," said Sarah, "I promise that I will help you get your revenge."

"I no longer desire vengeance," said the monster. "Our struggle has been too long for that, a simple end will suffice."

"Then that's what you'll have. We'll make sure of it."

Serenity was an odd place in that it had no suburbs and no urban sprawl, the city began at one point and ended at another, an Art Deco masterpiece rebuilt after the great earthquake; beyond that were fields to the north and south, mountains to the west, prairie to the east, and a river that ran through the center of town. While most modern American locales lived and died by the construction of the freeway system in the 50s and 60s, Serenity had thrived despite never being close to a thoroughfare, and never having any major industry to speak of. Magic was what flowed through the place and for centuries it had gathered artists, writers, thinkers and liars to its doorstep.

From miles away the bright lights of the Metropolis of the Midwest looked liked a beacon of hope to the weary traveler, even Karl Hesse, the weary immortal looked at them with fondness.

"How do we get down to the lost city?" Asked the monster.

"Like all good and creepy things, through a secret passageway," said Sarah. "This one's in the center of a crypt, a staircase carved out of the earth that leads all the way to the old city, hidden underneath the sarcophagus of a famous supernatural archeologist with an overdeveloped flair for the cheesy dramatic."

"Whose grave is it?"

"Guy named Elias Kord that died here in the 50s."

"I knew him a bit," said the monster. "We met inside a haberdashery in Cairo during the Ancient Egyptian craze of the early 20s, I was in dire need of a button for my cavalry jacket, if I recall correctly. Howard Carter had recently discovered Tutankhamen's tomb and Elias was mad for mummys, then again, so was the entire world at that point."

"I've heard various accounts of the man," said Sarah. "His crypt should be real a tourist attraction in this city, but it never is, everyone steers clear. The facts about him contradict each other, some make him out to be a crusader for the good guys and others paint him as a bit of a nefarious fool. What was he actually like?"

"Like most things, the truth is probably found somewhere between the two, when I met him, Elias was a bright young man with an interest in mythology and the occult, genuinely wide eyed and curious about a world that so few people take the time to see. He was somewhat of a rarity, a fearless American cowboy surrounded by his more restrained European colleagues, we shared an adventure in the desert, stopping the Acolytes of Anubis from unleashing their deity upon this reality again. Afterwards I'd hear mention of him but nothing substantial, some claimed that he fell in with Aleister Crowley and his lot, others that Elias had gathered allies and that he waged a silent war against them for over two decades. I had no idea that he had met his fate here in Serenity, I wish I could have spoken to him again. The world holds precious few mysteries for me any longer and I admit that the life and death of Elias Kord is one of them."

Sarah pulled the Waggoneer into a parking spot on the eastern edge of the cemetery, both she and Colonel Hesse took their respective stockpiles of weapons with them as they set foot inside the grounds through a rusty iron gate in need of repair. Without delay they found the place they were looking for. Twisted metal and chipped granite adorned the entrance to Elias Kord's crypt, his tomb was also on the east side of the Elysium Cemetery a few rows off from the gated entrance and difficult to miss; a large metal fence surrounded the structure and four ten foot tall carved stone obelisks stood sentry at each of the corners of an enormous granite pyramid with a burnished steel door on the south side. The door had been torn off of its hinges and was lying propped up against the building's side, bedlam greeted them as they entered the tomb, the sarcophagus had been smashed to reveal the hidden tunnel to the lost city beneath it, his wrapped body discarded on the floor near the far right corner.

Frankenstein's Monster went over to him, straightened his body and placed his arms on his chest so that they crossed. "I'm sorry, Elias. Lord and time willing, I will see to it that you are put to rest again."

"Assholes," said Sarah. "They didn't even try to look for the lever in the wall that moves the sarcophagus, they just wrecked everything without a care."

"The good doctor and his servants never were the nicest of grave robbers."

"Now I'm pissed, let's go beat him up."

"Outstanding idea."

"I thought so."

"How long will the descent take?" He asked.

"About two hours, maybe a little longer, I hope, I've only been down there once," said Sarah. "It's not exactly a direct route, the old city's buried hundreds of feet below us, there are other caverns to get through, a lot of climbing down and then back up to go back down again on the other side. Ready for some fun?"

"Always," said the monster.

The passageway was hewn from the unnatural solid bedrock that separated the buried city from the world above,

what was once dirt and river rock had been transformed into a solid mass of hardened stone following the wizard battle between Malvolio and Caledon in 1905. It was a narrow hole in the ground and not too tall, Colonel Hesse often needed to duck his head and squeeze his broad shoulders through sections, the angle of descent shifting from slight to steep with no warning. It was an arduous journey for both of them, by the time two
hours passed they weren't even halfway there yet, and Sarah's daughter had ceased being human.

*****

Attacking the game with a team of zombie football players had been a rousing success, the chaos from all of the panic and death had provided an abundance of magical fuel for the great machine, the Kirby lights on the panels pulsated at seemingly random intervals and the mechanisms inside of it hummed and whirred as they spun into action. It sat outside the doors of the old church the mad doctor used to conduct his experiments; an eight foot tall behemoth sewn together with two bodies guarded it, each of his limbs and his torso were elongated from the addition of another set of bones and musculature, and on his misshapen shoulders rested an extra head, which appeared to be dozing while the other kept watch.

Inside of the desecrated house of worship Victor Frankenstein was busy operating on a body that had been taken apart, the arms and legs, removed from the rest of a young woman's corpse were laying in bucket beside the doctor's feet. The maker of monsters looked worried, he pulled his blood soaked hands out of the cadaver on the table and removed his surgical mask, then pausing, he blew out an exasperated breath and ran his sanguine fingers through his gray streaked hair, leaving a reddish trail from the top of his forehead and along his mane to the scalp below.

His servant, Samuel, smoking a pipe, leaned against the back wall underneath an effigy of Christ, the red embers inside the meerschaum bowl glowing in the shadows as he puffed away. The smoke, with it's hearty aroma drifted up to the tall ceiling where it lingered like a gray storm cloud. "Master?"

The doctor cocked his ear to the side, listening to distant whispers in the air. "My son has come for a visit," he said. "We should prepare for his arrival." Leaving the operating table he walked from inside of the old sunken church through the large wooden front doors to the subterranean expanse outside, knocking the remains from his pipe, Samuel followed. Each time Victor Frankenstein saw the cavern, it was a wonder to behold. The wizard battle of 1905 and the earthquake that resulted had left something unique behind, a lost city; a mile wide in each direction, shaped like an auditorium with a tall stone ceiling and all of it was buried hundreds of feet below the surface. Few knew that it existed, fewer still knew how to reach it, and of those only a handful would dare to visit. He rested his right hand on a stack of bodies and drummed his fingers. Barrrump barrrump barrrump. "A pity, if only I had a little more time."

"What are your wishes?" Asked Samuel.

"Prepare the machine. It's early but we have little choice, they must all be awakened now."

"Yes, master."

"And once he is here, you will open the vault. I would like for my son to meet some of his younger siblings. Take charge of this, your other half will lead them."

"Of course, I'll begin the preparations." Samuel hobbled off to the far side of the great machine, dragging his bad foot and making a TAP TAP TAP sound with his cane as he went. Once there he whispered to it, subtle and slight, in a tongue not spoken by men since before the last ice age. And the machine listened.

The uneven floor of the cavern was covered with corpses, stacked three or four high in places like firewood for want of more room. Victor Frankenstein moved through the narrow rows of bodies passing his hands over them and reciting incantations in old Low German, he was followed by nine chemical warlocks who he placed at intervals of sixty feet apart throughout, once there they each continued to recite a specific part of the spell that they had been told, and who along with him at the top formed the points and apexes of a drawn pentagram. Eyes snapped open, bodies twitched and moved, guttural noises called out, the dead rose again.

They covered the whole cavern floor as they staggered about, their feet shuffling in small movements as they regained control of their withered muscles, their groans filled the auditorium and reverberated against the stone ceiling, growing louder and louder. Anarchy ensued as the creatures turned against one another, clawing and hitting and biting, they tried to tear each other apart, until the doctor began to sing *Parsifal* by Richard Wagner. The necromancer had a bewitching voice, the dead immediately ceased what they were doing and gave him their full attention. Victor Frankenstein continued to croon as the zombie audience stared and swayed, his chemical warlocks joined him, the nine that had cast the spell with him and another thirteen who had been watching from the sidelines. They added their voices to his and brought the unfortunate souls before them under their control, singing louder and louder, building to a crescendo of dazzling brilliance.

"And now my children," said the doctor. "It is time for you to murder a city."

Sarah and Colonel Hesse emerged from the passageway into the underground city sometime during the finale of *Parsifal.* "Yowzers," said Sarah. "The doc might be an evil tool but he sure can carry a tune."

"No doubt the result of another Faustian agreement." The monster brought forth his battleaxe and gripped it tight with both hands. "Come, we must end this before Wagner is ruined for me forever." Barrels full of majeesh lined the edge of the underground city, laid out like bowling pins, Colonel Hesse announced his assault by tossing a grenade, destroying them all.

Behind the church was a large metal vault about the same size and dimensions of a boxcar, welded together from numerous pieces of steel, it had a heavy door that swung out on hinges, but no lock, handle, or means of being opened apparent to the naked eye. Samuel passed his hand over the front of it and uttered another phrase in Low German, **"Apen nu."** The door opened, revealing the horrors within, misshapen monsters pierced together and brought back to life by Doctor Frankenstein poured out of the steel prison. Ten altogether; tall, short, wide, skinny, male, female; it didn't matter who they had been , affronts to nature and God was what they had all been turned into. One woman had another jaw sewn beneath her first and both appeared to be talking, a twelve foot tall male behemoth had six arms and a face that had been surgically implanted into the middle of his chest, another man had eight legs, six extra pairs grafted to three extra midsections like a centipede. And the rest were just as fantastic, monstrosities cobbled together by the mad scientist from dozens of bodies, his obedient and bizarre masterpieces to be unleashed upon his rebellious first born son.

Samuel eyed each of them with disdain, and then his body started to stretch and contort, his limbs grew and his skin peeled off, his hair fell out and he removed his nose with his hand, discarding the cartilage, and his mouth widened, showing the needlelike teeth inside. Where a man stood leaning against his cane seconds ago, now lurked a creature of ferocious power and strength whose kind had perished long before the great flood. He stepped towards the doctors creations and they recoiled in fear. The snake man beckoned them to follow him with a wave of his hand. "Thisss way." He and the doctor's new monstrosities circled around the church and most of the zombies where they blocked Sarah and Colonel Hesse's path before they had the opportunity to confront their intended target.

"You go get your evil pseudo dad," said Sarah. "I'll hold these guys off for a while." She winked and then waded into battle, her warhammer held aloft. "Holy frakkin' Lovecraft, you guys are ugly," said Sarah. "Seriously, did Herbert West put you guys together on a dare?" In her mind, Doombringer always sounded like the drums of war when she used it, a weapon of power that bonded with the user and encouraged them to victory and to more bloodshed. Sarah, the Huntress made quick work of the ones foolish enough to attack her.

Doctor Frankenstein gathered the chemical warlocks and most the zombies in front of the church and the great machine, he placed his hands on a panel of lights and switches and began to recite an incantation in Low German. A kaleidoscope of color and a raucous symphony of sound burst from the machine, enveloping everything before it, the entire underground city trembled as the villain and his monsters disappeared. The doctor called out over the cacophony as he and the others faded into the ether. "Auf Wiedersehen, mein Sohn!"

With his giant battleaxe in hand, Colonel Hesse leaped over the snake man and the rest of the madman's experiments towards the doctor and the great machine; the crash of metal on bedrock rang out as he landed a moment too late, Doctor Frankenstein was gone, along with everyone and everything else, including a third of the church.

"Das arschloch!" Shouted Frankenstein's Monster.

"Damn it." Said Sarah. Half of the new Frankensteins had been destroyed but the others were now running in the opposite direction at the Colonel, she shouted over the remaining bad guys to him. "Colonel, we need to get the hell out of here! If they're all topside, the city is screwed!

Most of the bad guys had disappeared but between the two of them there still remained the worst of the worst, the doctor's most dangerous fiends; the snake man, five leftover junior Frankensteins, and about a hundred rabid zombies. The monster of legend cracked the joints in his neck, drew his broadsword from its scabbard, and with it in his right hand and the battleaxe in his left, he said, "I'll meet you in the middle."

Sarah cut through the mass of walking dead in front of her like a surgeon through a cold cadaver, her blows with Doombringer were quick and precise, using the hammer half she caved their skulls in and on the return strike she sliced the tops of their heads off with the axe side of her weapon. From the corner of her eye she saw a group of zombies try to swarm her, she took the first one's head off with a golf swing, sending it flying fifty yards into the wall of a sunken building where it made a satisfying SPLAT. The others dog piled on top of her and managed to knock Doombringer out of her hands, where it was lost mere yards away in the confusion. Like someone being held under water, she burst through the battery of things holding her down and flung them back several feet.

Fatigued and hurting from head to toe, she stood there breathing heavily for a moment, covered in gore, while the zombies circled. "Fine, I'll just have to beat all of you to death again with my bare hands." Sarah used her super human strength to punch a hole through the middle of the nearest zombie's head. Fists and feet flew in a sudden choreographed dance of death as she decimated the remaining creatures. With her fight over and seeing Colonel Hesse still surrounded, she retrieved the warhammer and set out to help him defeat the rest of his sparring partners.

As Frankenstein's Monster buried his axe into the head of one of his younger siblings, he cut another in two with his broadsword, only the snake man and the poor soul with the head in his torso were left. Head/Torso guy tried to retreat and met Sarah as he made a break for it, she used the axe half of her weapon to slice him down the middle; spilling guts, brains and all onto the ground.

"Okay, that is just extra gross," she said.

With only one minion left they turned their attention to Samuel. "I have known this one a long time as well," said the noble monster. "A willing abettor to evil, fool that sold his soul to a minor demon and then pledged himself to Victor Frankenstein for protection." Karl Hesse raised his sword in mock salute. "Hello Igor."

The servant backed away green flame erupted from the mouth of the snake man, streaking upwards to the stone ceiling where it ignited a dozen sticks of dynamite wedged into the rocks. A chain reaction began in the center of the cavern's roof and spread out to more sticks of explosive placed throughout, the whole underground city shook and the noise was deafening, giant slabs of rock slipped from above and rained down on top of them.

Sunken buildings were being crushed all around and Sammy the snake man had disappeared from sight. "Huntress!" Bellowed the monster. He sprinted from a dozen yards away and smashed a falling piece of the stone ceiling right before it crushed Sarah.

"Run for the passageway!" She yelled.

"No time! Take my hand!" It was the last thing Sarah heard before she felt his fingers cover hers and the darkness consume them.

Chapter 9: Over the Rainbow

"Welcome to Avalon!" Cried Merlyn with his arms wide open as he smiled with a big pseudo-evil grin on his face. Hannah felt an odd tingling throughout her body, like a small electrical current was dancing across her skin. Whether it was from the trip or the destination she couldn't be sure. "Don't worry, that'll pass in a minute or two."

"What's that?" Asked Hannah.

"The body buzz you're feeling , it's essentially the equivalent of your ears popping when you land in an airplane. But in this case that's the sensation you feel when you make a cross-dimensional jump."

"So it's like my body knows that I'm not in the same universe. The frequency's been changed."

"Exactly," said Merlyn.

"Well that's just terrific," said Hannah. "Fine. Okay. Out with your wizard-splainy exposition, I know you're dying to. What the hell is Avalon? Other than the place King Arthur was taken when he died."

The wizard cleared his throat. "That's part of it, sure, but it's a lot bigger than only that. Avalon's a pocket dimension, created by The Twelve Science-Mages of ancient Highguard to protect and shelter the world's magic during the Fall of the Fourth Age of Atlantis."

"Really? That's your explanation," said Hannah exasperated. "Not helping. You just made everything way more complicated. I mean, that's like a whole other can of mythology you just opened."

"Fine (killjoy), I'll dumb it down for you," said Merlyn. "This is where the fairytales live, think less Hans Christian Anderson and more Shakespeare and the Brothers Grimm murdering Walt Disney in a ritual sacrifice kind of way. So enough questions, look around! You're in bloody parallel universe, lady."

Hannah began to actually look around and to take in the beauty and wonder of where she was. They were standing in the middle of a wide cobble stone road running through golden fields of wheat that stretched to the horizon, high above them twin suns shined on the land, yellow and red, the sky itself an aquamarine shade of green. In the distance the road continued on through a small village, but to Hannah's shock something spectacular loomed above the tiny town, a large castle floating hundreds of feet above the ground.

Polished black rocks had been fitted together in seem less precision to create the floating fortress, flowers of every color and variety adorned the windows, green-white vines and lavender creeping flock climbed up the walls to the very tops of the nine turrets. The castle itself rested atop an irregular square mile of earth suspended in midair, below it was a lake where a giant hole had been filled in by water from an underground aquifer. And between the two; rock, dirt, and toppled mason stone, hung, frozen in place as they tumbled down. It was as if a great hand had plucked the entire structure from the ground and left it in place, suspended in the air.

Although they could see the castle and the village in the distance, Hannah and Merlyn still had a long walk ahead of them. "Couldn't you have beamed us here a little closer?" Hannah asked. "Aren't we in a rush? Bad shenanigans happening back home and all that."

"Unfortunately no. This place is protected by big time wards, any closer and I'm afraid we could arrive with our insides on our outside." Said Merlyn. "And remember, don't worry about that too much, nice thing about parallel dimensions is that time works different in most places, we could spend days here and only a little while will have passed back on Earth."

"Oh, well at least there's that," said Hannah. "Which is to say, still freaking weird."

"Besides, I'd rather the locals didn't see me right from the get go. The last time I was here a Dhizen Demon followed me from one of the lesser Chinese hells, tore up the place bad before I could put it down. Some of the people who live in the village ahead threatened to rearrange my handsome face if I ever returned. Best we slip through and up to the castle quiet like."

"You are one heck of a fun date, Merlyn."

"Life of the party, that's me," he said.

Neither of them spoke for a long while after they started off for the castle and the village. At last Hannah reached out to hold his hand. "You know, I really need to say something.

I'm already smitten with impressive magical you, you don't have to always sound like the wise old professor." She stopped in the middle of the road, grabbed Merlyn's other hand and looked at his face, it wasn't only his eyes she gazed into but all of him, one of those soulful searches that takes in the whole person. "It's time for the secrets to fade away and for you to tell me everything."

"That could take a while," he said.

Gesturing to their surroundings Hannah said, "Apparently we have the time."

"I was… I was born during the apocalypse, every day of my life has been a fight for survival." Merlyn lowered his head. "I guess I never learned how to just talk to people."

"So why me and why now?" Asked Hannah.

"Because you're important to the future of your entire world. That's one thing both the histories of tomorrow and the prophecies of the past agree on. And they don't agree on much."

"Swear to god, Merlyn, if you call me the Chosen One I will punch you. Very hard. In sensitive places."

"Sorry," he paused. "But you really are the Chosen One, or at least one of them," said Merlyn. "Here's the rub though, you're just not the good guys' Chosen One."

Hannah was speechless. Her whole existence spinning out of control, she shook her head, went over to the side of the road and put her hands on her knees as she tried to get it together.

"You going to be okay?" Asked Merlyn.

"Yeah…yeah, y'know it's funny, even after the vampire thing and almost killing Kiran, it never occurred to me that I was going to end up being the bad guy."

"That's why I'm here, why we're here." He said pointing around. "I don't think it needs to be that way. What happens to you in the next few years will be a crux that the rest of the world will react to for another thousand years. You're a key figure in history, not the only one of course, but damn important. If we can change things now then maybe we can change all of it."

"That easy? Stop me from going all big bad and the scary future just fades away. Back To The Future rules and all, huh? " Said Hannah.

Merlyn did something unexpected then, he laughed. "Not exactly. When you're a chronomancer trying to prevent the apocalypse you tend to play the long game."

"This crap is so frustrating, why not show up earlier or just kill me and be done with it? Why even bother with all of this?"

"Doesn't work like that. Magic and science have one thing in common, they both require balance, nothing is ever really created or destroyed. It's just energies, remove them from one place and they'll only end up someplace else. Time travel's a lot like throwing a dart at a board, you can aim for the bullseye but that doesn't mean you're going to hit it every time." Merlyn smiled. "And I don't want to kill you. I knew that when I saw you save that family in the alley."

"Well, at least you don't want me dead," said Hannah. Merlyn didn't say anything, he simply grinned, shook his head no and continued towards the village.

As they walked they discovered they weren't alone on the road. Ahead of them a man and a woman dressed like two Puritans off of the Mayflower pulled a cart with a child inside of it; the toddler was wearing a bear costume but her/his little cherub face was exposed, the couple wore masks, the cheap plastic kind with the rubber band that went around the back, she wore a fox mask and he wore a wolf's. They were a family of predators.

"What are those things?" Asked Hannah in a quiet voice.

"Predator spirits, what some myths and stories call ghouls," said Merlyn. "The echoes of violent acts that have been cast into the void and have somehow landed here."

"Are they dangerous?" She asked.

"Sometimes, they're not very strong but they get really determined if you piss them off. If we stay calm and pass without drawing attention to ourselves we should be okay."

"Why do they look like a bunch of pilgrims on their way to a Halloween party?".

"I have no idea."

"Really," said Hannah as she side eyed Merlyn.

"What?" He said. "I'm not a magic eight ball, you know, there are still a few things that even I'm not aware of."

"I. Am. Shocked." She said. "Terrifically shocked and delighted. There's stuff that even the mighty Merlyn doesn't know about. There's hope for the rest of us yet."

"Hardy har. That's very funny, laugh it up lady."

An abrupt halt came to their light hearted banter as the bear-child turned around in the little cart ahead to look at them. But it's face had changed, instead of a toddler's it looked like a bear cub's skull, bits of flesh hanging off the bone, tiny red lights shimmered in the recesses of its eye sockets, and it was snarling at them in a barely audible tone. "Um," said Hannah, "you didn't mention that these things were god awful terrifying up close."

"Yeah," whispered Merlyn. "That would be one of the things I wasn't too familiar with, I've never actually encountered a ghoul before."

"Awesome. At least you don't have ghouls in the stupid apocalypse."

"No, we had far worse," he said. "Just, y'know, keep cool, and please don't vamp out."

"Are you freaking kidding me? Vamp out? I'm about ready to pee my pants."

A murder of crows gathered on an old wooden fence half fallen into the field on their right, the murder was making a racket; they cawed, they screeched, they shrieked, they beat their wings and they pecked; all to a chorus of calamity and cantankerous caterwauling. The family of ghouls' attention was now fully focused on Hannah and Merlyn, mom and dad removed their masks, discarding them in the cart. Beneath the façade was horror, the true faces of a fox and a wolf stared at them, all of their skin and fur had been removed. Taut red muscle and white strings of sinew stretched against bone while dark globs of blood bubbled and dripped from the below the seams of flesh onto the dirt and rocks of the worn road.

"I have maybe enough juice left to deal with one of them," said Merlyn.

The father-wolf was the first to attack, he rushed towards them on all fours, kicking up a cloud of dust behind him and making a clickety clack noise against the stones as the claws on his hands and bare feet met the surface.

"You deal with dad, I'll take care of mom and junior," said Hannah. Before Merlyn could answer she drew her butterfly swords out of the crisscrossed scabbards on her back and darted into the wheat field on the right hand side of the road.

Merlyn laughed to himself. "Lady with a plan," he said aloud. Crouching down he felt the road with the palm of his hand, he mouthed a spell and the ground began to shake; rocks dislodged from their setting and bounced around like Mexican jumping beans, dirt stirred and rose into the air, the street before him whipped like a rope; the raised wave of earth rushed ahead until it met the ghoul where it crashed over him and dragged him deep beneath the surface.

Witnessing the demise of her mate the Mother-Fox let out a deafening shriek. Hannah flanked her from the field and leaped out to confront her, the Dragon Blade stretched out in her right hand and the Phoenix Sword reversed in her left, held in a defensive position to her side. Swinging down she severed both of the ghouls hands at the wrists, and then pivoting up with the other blade she split the howling thing in two from crotch to cranium. Hannah heard skittering and rustling, she kept her swords down and looked from side to side trying to find where junior had gone. "Where the fuck are you, you little creep?" She whispered.

Merlyn joined her, panting, out of breath and with his hands on his knees. Eyeing the two halves of the mother he said, "You get the kid?"

"Does it look like I got him?" She said. Listening close, Hannah picked up something moving to her left and flicked the Phoenix Blade out in its direction. "Little bastard's over there," she pointed.

"Flush him out," said Merlyn. "Then get far out of the way, I'll do the rest."

"I am not your hunting dog," she responded.

"Just do it please." He said.

"Hush now, dear Merlyn." Hannah closed her eyes and listened, the breeze stirred the stalks of wheat causing them to sway back and forth in the fields, and off in the distance the sound of wind chimes greeted them. The Phoenix and Dragon etchings on the swords began to move, the mythical creatures appeared to come alive, and started to glow, then burst into red and green flames that covered the length of the blades. Out of the field the bear cub ghoul jumped into the air screaming, claws raised and teeth bared towards Hannah's head, she sidestepped away, swinging the crimson sword afire and cut the little beast from his belly to the ribs on his left side, spilling his insides on the ground and setting him on fire as he landed. Standing over its body Hannah watched the fire consume the little ghoul with haste, leaving nothing but a pile of charred ashes lying on the ground, being picked up and scattered to the countryside by the breeze. The fire surrounding the swords went out quick in a sudden flicker as Hannah lowered them to her sides.

"What the hell?" Said Merlyn. His eyes were as wide as plates and he was as confused as he had ever looked to her.

"Pretty cool, huh?" Said Hannah. "The swords feel at home here, I could hear them singing in my head and my heart. Like the spells they were forged with think of this place as kindred."

"Think?" He asked.

"Of course," she said. "They're alive, didn't you know that? I mean, not like people, but the dragon and the phoenix carvings on the blades are conscious in and of themselves, like really smart pets, the type that are faithful companions to people I suppose."

"Well, I'll be damned, I wasn't expecting anything like that," said Merlyn. "Best estate sale find ever."

"Uh huh," said Hannah. "Someday you're going to tell me where you really got these."

"Someday. Come on, let's get into town before we make any more new friends."

Hannah put the swords away and they set off down the road again, after about a minute Merlyn started to whistle and Hannah began to sing, *We're Off To See The Wizard*. There was no skipping.

Hannah The Huntress

*****

"Welcome to Geris Al Dem," said Merlyn pointing to the dilapidated town.

"This place is a ruin," Hannah proclaimed as they walked into town. The shadow of the castle covered the entire place; the twin suns overhead were fixed in the sky, positioned at perfect angles so that the darkness would always fall below.

Two streets paved with stones ran through the little village below the castle in the sky, meeting at a crossroads in the middle, dilapidated buildings constructed from brick and mortar with wooden shingle roofs lined each. Almost everything appeared to be coming apart; the walls sagged and fell in places, bricks spilled into the road, weeds choked the front of most of the buildings, the windows were either dirty or broken, and the few structures that weren't falling down had nearly been destroyed by fire, their charred remains left to deteriorate until they were gone. Even the air smelled bad, full of dirt and dust and rot. Nobody alive was left in the hamlet, but an ominous presence still lingered, Merlyn could feel it. "We should leave," he said to Hannah.

Without speaking they walked through the center of town and kept moving until they were well past the final building. "That was weird," said Hannah. "It was like a shroud of depression and anxiety was thrown over me for a minute there. All I wanted to do was get out."

"I felt the same," said Merlyn. "I think it was literally the shadow of the castle which created it, there's some kind of spell, some malevolence at work back there. Let's keep going a ways, we need to figure out how to get up to the castle."

"How'd you get up there last time?"

"Hot air balloon. This area used to be full of them, all bright and beautiful, they were how the locals used to travel long distances. I paid a guy, he took me up, pretty easy. Honestly that's how I figured we'd get up there this time."

"I don't think we're going to find anything like that this time," said Hannah. "From the way that town felt I'm guessing everyone who could leave did so as fast as they could."

About a mile to the north of Geris Al Dem a stream from the lake below the castle cut through the road, a hundred foot bridge curved over the top of it and on the other side rested an inn. Unlike the buildings in town this one was in terrific condition and made of solid oak logs fitted together like the mightiest of Lincoln cabins. They went inside, the building was two stories tall, had three bedrooms, and great room with five tables, a bar with six stools, and a large kitchen. Compared to town the inn was a palace, albeit an empty one.

"Jesus," said Hannah. "This place just gets weirder and weirder."

Hannah sat down at one of the tables and Merlyn ducked back behind the bar. "Want a beer?" He asked.

"It's illegal to ply underage women with booze, Mr. Wizard."

"Was that a yes?"

"Yes."

The wizard returned to the table and set down two frosty glass bottles with dark amber liquid inside of them, Merlyn smacked his against the edge of the table to knock the foam off and took a long satisfying drink. "Mmm, pretty damn good, nice and cold too. Ice chest's still full, someone was here not long ago."

"Not much dust either." Hannah ran her finger across the surface of the table and held it up. "Maybe two or three days at the most." Taking her thumb she flicked the cap off of her beer and lifted it to her lips. "Blech," she said wrinkling her nose and sticking her tongue out.

"Not a fan of interdimensional micro brews?" He said.

"Meh, I'm more of a Budweiser gal than a craft beer snob." She said as she downed the rest of her beverage in one long gulp and set it on the table triumphantly.

"Bloody savage," said the wizard. He scooted back, put his feet on the table and drank his beer in silent contemplation for a few minutes. "Shit, I got nothing. Any ideas on how we can get up there?"

"Yes, actually. How about you do that thing with the ground again and build us an elevator to the castle. Think you could pull that off?"

Merlyn slapped his knee with his free hand and exclaimed, "That is brilliant! I'm going to go get another beer and then we're off!"

Half an hour later Hannah and Merlyn were standing in a field underneath what appeared to be the gated side of the castle, from what they could see there was just enough of a ledge for them to stand on once the got up there. Merlyn was hiccupping, and slightly drunk.

"Need more liquid courage?" Asked Hannah. "The hell, wizard boy? I've watched you fight things without a second thought that most people would run screaming away from."

"I hate heights," he said.

"Don't worry, if you fall I'll catch you."

"I wouldn't doubt it for a second. All right, let's do this." Merlyn knelt down to the ground and started to tap it, well, play it like a set of skins with his Bonham drumsticks. He muttered to himself for a bit and then got louder and louder until he stood up with his arms outstretched and shouted, **"Terra consurget, terra consurget, TERRA CONSURGET!"**

The ground trembled as the column of earth rose into the air, the ascension was startling and fast, the wind rushed to meet them, pushing them down against the surface, the landscape below resembled a toy diorama within mere seconds. The dirt elevator was six feet in diameter but with an uneven surface, it was difficult for Hannah and Merlyn to maintain their footing, so they held onto each other for dear life. As sudden as the climb was the stop was even more jarring, the halt itself near pitched the two of them off the side to the ground below, and worst of all the column was a good ten feet away from the ledge of the floating castle and the gated entrance.

"Son of a bitch," he said.

"Hold on, Mr. Wizard." Hannah grabbed Merlyn tight across the middle, backed up a few steps and then with a running start jumped with him from the column of earth onto the ledge of the castle in the sky. They landed in an awkward sprawl with Hannah on top and both of their heads banging into the gate.

"OW!" They exclaimed with simultaneous and painful precision.

Hannah twisted around and pulled on the gate. Nothing happened. "Um, how do we get in?" Soon as the words were out of her mouth the gate started to swing open to the interior of the castle grounds. "Nope, nothing weird going on here at all. No, sir."

"Do you not watch horror movies, woman?" Said Merlyn.

"Shush, you," she said.

"Come on," said Merlyn as they both stood up and brushed themselves off. "Let's go find the creepy ass landlord."

They entered the castle grounds and Hannah immediately had to cover her mouth to stop from shrieking in pure terror. "What the bloody hell is all of this?"

"This…this wasn't supposed to be like this, this wasn't here last time." He said.

"Well, what do we do now, fight or flight?" She asked.

"Probably both, but we're here, we keep going." He said.

"Oh great, that sounds just awesome," replied Hannah.

The courtyard was decorated with row after row of crucified men, women and children; their bodies flayed open and rotting under the heat of the suns. The air was heavy and humid, and it stank like death, flies buzzed all about, everywhere, Hannah and Merlyn covered their mouths to keep from breathing them in. Maggots covered the bodies, devouring the flesh, and another murder of crows circled above, diving and landing on the bodies, tearing meat off of bones and flying away again, taking their turn at the buffet.

The wizard and the girl crossed the horrible landscape with haste and came to the doors to the fortress, wooden wonders made by hand, ten feet tall, bedecked with scenes of warfare. As Merlyn approached to knock they began to open, slow and without sound; stepping inside both Hannah and he were taken aback at the splendor of the place, enormous was an ill fitting description for a structure so vast containing space that seemed to go on and on. But the place itself paled before the beauty of the woman standing before them in the center of the massive floor. Merlyn cleared his throat and exchanged subtle nods with the lady of the manor, addressing Hannah he said, "This is Castle Arithem.

Allow me to introduce you to your future self, evil hybrid vampire Hannah."

"Hello, me," said tomorrow Hannah as she smiled wickedly at her younger self.

Chapter 10: The League of Sidekicks

Matt and Zeke carried body after body out of the fallen office building, chalk white cinder blocks lined the entrance like crooked teeth, the air on the ground was choked thick with dust and debris, while overhead the haze was punctuated by colorful fireworks exploding in a delightful display of mirth and jubilation. The city had become an abattoir of psychedelic cacophony.

The dead were placed over to the side near the opening to the alley while the wounded were set in front along the sidewalk. Kiran and Cassie did what they could for the injured, bandaging wounds, holding hands, and all while trying to provide comforting words to a dozen or so scared and hurting people.

"Where the hell are the paramedics and the police? Shouldn't they be here somewhere close with all of the earthquake damage?" Said Cassie. Her hushed voice directed right at Kiran's ear so to not upset anyone.

"You'd think so," said Kiran. "That's the frightening thing, if they aren't here or nearby then that means things are even worse somewhere else."

Cassie tugged on Kiran's shirt and pointed upwards. "Or maybe they can't come, someone might be stopping them. I don't want to know what kind of a-hole's lighting off fireworks like it's a Fourth of July celebration."

"Yeah, that's a cheerful thought," said Kiran.

"And they seem to be getting closer too," said Cassie.

154

The boys brought out a middle aged man in a light suit and tie, and set him down, his femur bone was broken in several places and sticking out of his pant leg in two spots; by his knee and the bottom of his calf, his blood had soaked through the clothing, changing it from a summer tan to a rust red that ran from the top of the thigh all the way down to his foot. Zeke had a sick look on his face as he and Matt lowered him to the ground. "Thank god this guy's passed out, I've seen a couple of breaks before while playing sports but that is particularly gnarly."

They heard the stomp and shuffle of the zombies' feet before they saw them marching up the block. A riot of the dead that got louder as they got nearer, they scratched and groaned, slished and moaned, wailed and flailed, grrrddd and arrrghed, and then, as if prodded by some invisible whip they started running towards them. Desiccated corpses wearing their Sunday finest barreling in their direction as fast as they could. About twenty were in the group; men, women, even a child or two, they all looked like families gone to church, not ashen and swollen bodies taken out of their graves.

"Sweet baby Jesus help us," muttered Zeke. "Everybody grab someone, we have to get inside now!"

"The hell?" Said Cassie. Turning around she saw the dead coming towards them and screamed, then with Kiran's help they picked up the man with the busted leg and tried to drag him into the coffee shop next to them.

The kids tried to save as many people as they could but they failed, the mass of zombies were on them before they had a chance to get inside, they pulled the wounded right out of their arms and ripped them limb to limb in front of them. Terrified but alert and working in unison the four friends closed and locked the door, grabbed the overturned furniture and anything they could find lying around and barricaded themselves in. It was a miracle the large windows had survived the quake, they were at least an inch thick and had several cracks but they were still standing, they piled boxes and display racks next to them in case they were broken and the creatures started to get in.

"Oh God," said Cassie. "I think I'm going to throw up."

It smelled like coffee and blood, thick and metallic, a heavy scent that lingered in the air long after whatever caused it was over. They watched the carnage unravel from the false safety of the ruined shop. The zombies tore apart everyone that they had laid down on the sidewalk moments before, the injured and the dead alike; they ripped off limbs, and they disemboweled the living with their fingernails, digging into the flesh until it split after it couldn't stretch any further, and they ate them.

"We need to get out of here and as far away as possible, those windows aren't going to hold up forever," said Kiran.

"The observatory," said Matt. "It's probably the only safe place left, we leave out the back through the alley and then make a run for it. Those things are a little faster than Romero zombies but not that much, we can beat them."

"Solid plan, we get there and wait for our superhero and wizard to get the hell back from their immensely ill timed other dimensional walkabout." Kiran went to the back door, opened it and looked out. "All right, gang, coast is clear, everyone grab something heavy to hit dead assholes with and let's go." As they each picked up something to hit the zombies with the storefront window was smashed open and the dead began to pour into the coffee shop. Opening the door again and running through, Kiran shouted, "Go go go!"

*****

The heavy metal door banged shut behind Kiran as she and the others ran into the alley, startled by the sound she looked back and was terror-stricken that she didn't see Matt, he should have followed them right through. "Matt!" She yelled.

"What's wrong?" Asked Cassie. And then realizing the what, she said, "Where's Matt?"

Kiran pulled on the door handle, desperate to get it to open. "It just shut all of a sudden, Matt's still on the other side, with them. This thing isn't budging, help me pull."

They both dropped the chair legs they'd taken out of the shop and began to pull on the handle as hard as they could with both hands; they pulled, they kicked, they hit and still it wouldn't move. Meanwhile Zeke had found a slender chunk of wood from a broken down palette and had wedged it into the gap between the door and frame in an attempt to get it open. Still nothing.

"Oh god, he's going to die," said Kiran. She fell to her knees in frustration and hammered on the door with both fists, the metal made a hollow clanging noise with each strike. "Those things will tear him apart. We have to get back in there, we need to run back around to the front."

Cassie tapped her on the shoulder and pointed down the alley, two of the rotting creatures were coming towards them, they had a shambling gait but that didn't stop them from moving at a quick pace. "Not to be insensitive but right now we have our own problems."

"There's only two of them," said Zeke. "We can take these things." Both he and Cassie picked up a broken piece of wood off of the palette nearby and charged the things. Cassie tackled a rather dapper zombie in a tuxedo, driving him to the pavement and proceeded to bash his brains in, Zeke met his head on, a burly fresh corpse that was dressed like a trucker and that refused to topple over. "Fall down, you rotten dead son of a bitch."

Cassie glanced up from bashing the tuxedo zombie's skull in with the discarded cast iron skillet, Zeke had sunk a foot long pointed piece of lumber into his creature's chest but it was still moving towards him. He looked flustered. "It's not a vampire, you have to get the brain!" She yelled.

"Oh yeah, right, duh, I got 'em turned around in my head." Zeke ran back, picked up another piece of jagged wood from the pile of disassembled pallets, ran forward, and stabbed it through the burly zombie's left eye socket until it hit the brain." The thing sputtered from side to side and then keeled over like a knocked out cartoon character. Huffing and puffing with his hands on his knees, he grinned and gave Cassie a thumbs up.

The shy girl with the bright blue hair was covered in blood, brain, and other unspeakable gore. "Oh Jesus," she whispered.

Zeke went over and put his arms around her; he wiped the blood and guts off of her face with his t-shirt, touched her cheek, kissed her tears, and raised his right hand to receive a high five. "Come on, up high, that was fuggin' badass."

"You're such a dork." She slapped his hand and laughed as they got to their feet.

Not thirty seconds passed before more of the dead arrived, a lot more, so many that they choked the alley near the entrance to the coffee shop and Matt.

"We gotta go, now," said Zeke.

"No," said Kiran. "We have to go back for Matt." She looked warm and flushed, on the verge of sickness, sweat poured off of her and she was out of breath.

"I'm sorry, but we don't have a choice." He and Cassie took her by each arm and nudged her to start moving.

The mass of zombies forced them to run out the back of the alley and down the street several blocks where they ended up in an old industrial cul de sac. Parts of it had been turned into storefronts and eateries, wrecked and abandoned now because of the earthquake. A wide street opened into the dead end with a giant closed factory on the left side and an L shaped brick warehouse that took up the other two sides, they were trapped with no way out but the way they had come in. Desperation set in as dozens of zombies rushed onto the street, but then a strange thing happened, the creatures didn't run directly at them, they stopped and they waited, like animals on the hunt waiting for their handler's next command.

Gathered in the center of the street the three friends stood back to back to back, preparing themselves for the attack. "What the hell?" Said Cassie. "I mean, I'm no expert but aren't these things mindless? Y'know, the eat first and ask questions later lot."

"Remember what Merlyn told us," said Zeke. "Someone's controlling these things."

"Yeah, Doctor freaking Frankenstein, so we might be even more screwed than we thought." Said Kiran. "I guess that is, if you can get more screwed than horribly and brutally dead." Her voice was raspy and drifted off as she spoke.

Zeke's hand bumped hers and he flinched. "Oh wow, you're totally hot," he said.

Kiran gave him a look that would shrivel any man's testicles. "Really. You think this is the time to hit on me? And in front of Cassie, what will the zombies think?"

"No," said Cassie turning around. "You're honest to God on fire, look!"

Tilting her head down, Kiran gasped at her hands as she saw the flames dance across her fingertips, smoke started to rise off of her skin and it was hot to the touch, her black hair had strands of fire throughout, and in her mouth she tasted ashes. For a moment she was alarmed and in a panic, but then a soothing calm washed over her, she realized there wasn't any pain, in fact, now that the fire was being let out of her, she felt better than she had a few minutes ago. Kiran let the inferno build, covering her entire body, and still she felt nothing, even her clothes didn't burn, it was as if the fire was just a little beyond her touch but remained hers to control. "Stay behind me," she said.

Kiran held both of her arms out towards the oncoming mass of zombies and shouted, "Flame on, bitches!" A wall of fire ten feet tall and twenty feet wide erupted from where she was standing and spread down the alley, engulfing the lot of them. The heat was so hot that it went from yellow and red to blue and white, burning the flesh and muscle from the dead until only their charred bones were left crumbled on the asphalt.

"Holy shit!" Said Cassie and Zeke together. They were standing back a dozen yards, eyes wide and mouths agape, peeking from behind an overturned restaurant patio table at the zombie barbecue and their friend with the new Johnny Storm superpowers.

Kiran was beaming as the flames died out around her. "Seriously! On a scale of one to Evel Knievel, how cool was that?"

But their celebration was short, through the dark smoke a shadow appeared, the outline of a massive monster; tall and wide, with a large rifle in its hands, and whoever, whatever it was, was staring right at them, it's green eyes shining bright through the haze.

*****

The door to the alley slammed shut in front of Matt, trapping him inside with the zombies, he smelled their rotting flesh a second before one of them grabbed him by the throat and pulled him back a couple of steps. Prying the thing's hand off and turning around, Matt felt a wet drop on his neck and looked at his hand where he saw blood from being scratched. Panic flooded throughout him, the kind you get right before you decide whether to fight or flee; *they're not contagious, they're not contagious, that's what the wizard said,* he had to remind himself. That was all the time for worry that he had, the zombies rushed him as group, five of them grabbed him and pushed him back up against the door. They clawed and scratched and tore at him, one bit into his forearm as he attempted to move them back, another with her bottom jaw gone jumped on top of the pack and tried to tear his eyes out. Something about the fear and the stink ignited his senses, it brought to the surface a part of him that was adjacent to the person he usually was, not a thing that was hidden but a part of the self that resides one room over from the rest. He snarled at the goddamn monsters and then threw all of them off of him at once, like Neal Adam's Superman breaking his Kryptonite chains.

Five steps away Matt took the first zombie by the hair and pummeled his head into the ground so hard that his skull split open and his brain oozed out. The second and third zombie that came at him he crushed their heads together until they stopped moving, zombie number four he knocked over and kicked his brains in, and for five, he popped her cranium like a melon by squeezing both sides of her head together. Panting and out of breath, Matt found a chair and sat down, he held his hands out and looked at them; they were larger, hairier and had two inch claws on each finger. He dropped one hand to the tile floor and scraped his finger over it, the claw left a quarter inch deep mark in the stone. Raising his head he found his reflection in a chrome refrigerator lying on the floor not far from where he was sitting, in the image he recognized a beast better suited for a fairy tale than for a teenager. He was bigger than usual, at least over six foot compared to his normal five foot ten, where his clothes weren't stretched they had ripped to make room; his hair was longer, darker and thicker, and covered most of him from head to toe, except his face, there he found that his features were still smooth; but there were changes, beneath the long hair his ears were pointed and amongst his teeth he had larger fangs than Hannah did when she vamped out last night. *My eyes,* he thought, *thankfully they're still human, and my thoughts, I still think like a man and not an animal.*

As he sat there thinking to himself he began to smell something awful, it was patchouli. The rank odor wafted into the shop, offending his heightened senses near to the point of illness, and underneath it, being covered up by nature's foulest oils was the B.O. plenty of a funky hippie that hadn't bathed since bell bottoms went away. Matt got to his feet, he sniffed the air, bent at the midsection so that his back was humped over and held his clawed fists loosely in front of him anticipating trouble. A chemical warlock with dirty blonde dreadlocks hanging down to his waist, wearing khaki green cargo shorts and a tie dye t-shirt cackled at Matt as he crawled over the wreckage blocking the entrance to the coffee shop, slithering inside on his belly. He huffed and puffed in exertion from climbing the wreckage and then stood up glaring, all while wearing a rictus grin on his face. Glossy eyed, high as a kite and still laughing, he raised his hands like a maestro conducting an orchestra and directed them to the half standing wall behind Matt.

The madman pulled the side of the building down on top of him, it fell like a crashing wave, covering him in a tomb of clay and shale. It pulverized his legs and smashed his back, he tasted blood in his mouth and felt the warm sticky gore spread all over his body. He saw stars but not birdies, consciousness became precarious, his breathing became shallow and short, his pain ebbed from excruciating to nothing, until at last the light faded to darkness. And then he slipped out of his body and into the vision lands of the Witchery Way.

*****

The Queen of Dark Tomorrow walks on broken glass,
her soldiers are dead yet their weapons remain.
They watch the sunrise but walk in the night,
A Horde will descend upon the village.

Six serpents exiled will return with the dawn,
One will die again before the beginning.
Anointing the Queen in slaughter,
The Dragon King watches and waits.

Now I am become vengeance,
Shatterer of worlds of vertigo.
From beyond the event horizon,
The Blood of Merlyn will save us all.

You are dying in the light,
You are already dead on the ground.
You will survive in the spaces between,
You will live on in the Witchery Way forever.

Chapter 11: Broken Mirror

Hannah looked at Merlyn like she wanted to tear his head off. "This is the God damn lesson?" She asked.

"This is it. Know thy self, Hannah Harrison."

The foyer to Castle Arithem was a work of art; beautiful bright frescoes depicting foreign mythologies adorned the walls, the high ceiling was a lush stucco that resembled a cumulus cloud, the staircase was carved from white marble with swirls of brown and black, and the tile floor was arranged in sequences of mathematical designs. Evil future Hannah looked like a goddess, with marmoreal skin polished like a stone that shined beneath the sunlight streaming through the numerous windows with their clever mosaics, and lustrous black hair that hung to the middle of her back against her long sleeveless purple dress. A golden starburst was clasped next to her bosom and the left side was embroidered with a vine of green leaves from chest high to ankle low. Present Hannah stared in disbelief until her dark reflection spoke.

"Ah, wizard, how wonderful to see you again. And you've brought the most splendid of visitors. My thanks."

"Yeah, I'm playing the ghost of Christmas future on this trip," said Merlyn. "Nothing quite says, 'just say no to the dark side' like seeing how bat shit crazy-evil you're going to become."

"Oh, sweetums," said future Hannah. "You should see the bastard that you turn out to be, pot meet kettle."

Hannah screamed, "Both of you, shut the hell up!" She ran up to herself, an inch away from her own face, seized her shoulder with one hand and then with the other pointed to the courtyard. "Was that you? Did you murder all of those people?"

"Of course," replied the reflection. "And slowly, I prolonged their deaths for days, sometimes even weeks longer than necessary. I particularly enjoyed eating the children while listening to the parents beg for mercy. Did you know that a small child sounds almost the same as whining pig when it's frightened? Tastes almost the same too."

Hannah struck her future self with the back of her fist and sent her flying across the room until she landed like a cat on her feet near the far wall. "You hit like a girl," said evil Hannah from afar.

"Enough." Said Merlyn. "How did you get them up here? This place is your prison, you can't leave."

"Silly wizard. Even here I have friends and followers, they bring me snacks. And they bring me news from far away lands and times, it's funny the things you discover when you listen without all of the noise from the rest of the world."

"Say goodbye to your buffet, Vampirella, because on the way out I'm locking the doors for good." Said Merlyn.

"I thought Vampirella was a good guy," said Hannah.

"Got you there," said evil Hannah.

"Shut up. Both of you." Said Merlyn.

167

"Okay then, how about we skip over all of this posturing nonsense, I'm a monster and you know that, which is why you've brought the girl for this little Mirror Spock powwow." Future Hannah turned to her younger self and gestured to the stairs. "So why don't we go talk, and maybe then you can decide whether or not an evil goatee is the right look for you."

*****

Hannah sat across the table from herself, preparing for the *Interview with the Vampire* to begin, Merlyn remained downstairs. They were in a large room several stories up, the walls were constructed out of polished black stones, there was a big canopy bed covered with white furs and lavish pillows on one side of the room, and on the other side was a solid oak table with two heavy chairs next to an opening that looked out over the countryside south of town. To Hannah's surprise fresh flowers decorated the entire space; yellow daisies sat in a vase on top of a nightstand, purple irises covered the window box, and inside of a bowl sitting on the table half filled with water rested three white lilies; everything was quite beautiful.

"Oh this is just fucking perfect," said Hannah. Her tone was as dry and full of contempt as a nun's knickers. "I'm in a parallel dimension with my evil future self and an asshole wizard who I either want to murder or make sweet love to depending on what minute of the day it is."

"There's a solution to that," said evil future vampire Hannah. "It's called angry sex."

"Listen, evil vampire me, Jesus Christ. You know what?" Said Hannah. "This is too God damn confusing, I'm just going to call you Vannah from now on."

"I remember when I used to look at him that way. Some free advice," said Vannah. "Stop thinking with your vagina. That son of a bitch doesn't want to stop the apocalypse, he wants to win it."

"What do you know about him?" Hannah asked.

"Everything, we were constant companions for over a century, even as mortal enemies we still cared about one another." She paused for a second and played with her fingernails, then with her index finger she carved a picture of a heart into the table with a knife sticking out of it. "After all, love twisted like a knife in the heart is merely obsession."

Hannah thought about that for a moment and then nodded. "How long have you been here?" She asked.

"Difficult to say," said the vampire. "Time moves so slowly here and the suns never set, if I hazarded a guess, I'd suppose that it would have to be a quarter century since my jailer put me inside this place and lifted Castle Arithem into the sky. I think you can guess who that was."

"Merlyn."

"Oh yes, however not the one you know, the version that trapped me was older, the arch-wizard in his prime, a battle mage from the

Apocalypse Wars over a thousand years in the future. The puppy you travel with only learned that I was here a few months ago, by my count anyway, it's hard to keep track of the days when there are no nights. I've been waiting for you to show up ever since. We've come full circle, my dear."

"Do you remember all of this happening?" Asked Hannah.

"More or less," said Vannah. "You need to understand, for me, you, and right now was over 200 years ago. Seriously, do you even recall everything that you did last week?"

"Of course not, but then again I didn't travel to an interdimensional fairyland last week." Said Hannah.

"Touche," replied Vannah. "Yes, I remember all of it; feeding on Kiran, the guilt, Merlyn's magical fire that supposedly cleansed me, the coin, the fear, the ghouls, the town, the climb, the bodies, meeting me, this conversation. Every. Damn. Thing. I also remember fighting the thirst until it drove me to the edge of madness. I remember watching everyone I loved dying around me while I went on living. I remember the stink and the betrayal of human beings. I didn't turn to the darkness overnight, and not all at once. For over a century I tried to deny who I really was, but inch by inch, moment by moment I was losing. We are an undeniable force of nature, a part of something larger than ourselves, the blood demands it. Fight it or embrace it, but it does not matter; be it a day from now or in a hundred years, you will become me."

"The hell I will, Merlyn showed me all of this to give me a choice." Said Hannah. "And I choose the light over your spooky self-defeatist sermon any day."

"Oh, wait, you're so right, I see the error of my existence now. Thank you." Said Vannah. "Y'know, I think I was wearing a Sex Pistols shirt instead of The Clash when I made this little trip." She clapped her hands together and shouted, "Problem solved! Merlyn has saved you from a horrible future, I bet I'll be fading away ala Back to the Future time travel rules any second now."

"Two hundred years, a mess of evil crazy, and I'm still a snarky bitch when the situation is dire." Said Hannah. "What are you planning."

The vampire bared her teeth and laughed. "Why, to kill myself, of course. And the damn wizard that imprisoned me here." Her speed was blinding as she crossed the room, hands and claws outstretched in an effort to murder her younger self. Hannah attempted to dodge the fatal strike when she felt the mystical bomb go off, Vannah wasn't confronting her head on, she was attacking her with magic.

*****

The explosion shattered the heavy oak double doors to the evil vampire's sitting room, reducing the carved wooden masterpiece to splinters, and threw Hannah fifty feet down the hallway cart wheeling end over end until she landed on her butt smack in the middle of a large tile mosaic of a

171

hunter killing a bear with a bow and arrow. Upon hearing the calamity Merlyn came running up the stairs and down the passage until he stopped a dozen yards from Hannah, bewildered, and viewed the smoke and the fire from the direction of the sitting room rushing towards them. Through the blaze he could just make out the outline of a woman at the other side of the hall screaming at them, her voice distorted by the inferno, future evil hybrid vampire Hannah.

"Move!" She yelled. Present Hannah was already back on her feet and hauling ass down the corridor.

"What?" Said Merlyn. His expression and tone were equal parts alarm and sudden confusion.

"Move your butt, wizard boy!"

As soon as Hannah reached him she grabbed his arm and they set off through the castle down to the courtyard at a breakneck pace. Sensing her anxiety Merlyn started to run as fast as he could. Shouts of GOD DAMN IT, MERLYN and YOU FUCKING BITCH punctuated the hallways and followed them as they moved ass down the marble staircases through the bowels of the citadel.

"What the hell happened?" He asked.

"Evil future me tried to kill sweet present me so that she could kill current dumbass you." Said Hannah. "She really doesn't like you."

"Well that hardly seems fair, it's not like I locked her up in this place." He said. "Not yet anyway."

"Yeah, crazy her, she's under the impression that if she murders your ass now then she won't be locked up at all."

172

"That's ridiculous, time travel doesn't work like that, at best all she'd create would be an alternate timeline."

"Did you maybe get an impression the last time you were here that perhaps you weren't welcome?"

"There may have been some vague threats after she explained that I was the one who put her in here. Or will."

"Fantastic," said Hannah. "Next time a pissed off uber-bitch ex-girlfriend threatens you, please don't bring me along for the reunion."

"Ex-girlfriend?"

"Yeah, apparently we dated...er, future you and future me dated. Can't you just feel the love?"

"Any other revelations?" Merlyn asked.

"Yeah, don't become a psychotic asshole vampire. Lesson learned, professor. Happy?"

"Ecstatic," he beamed as they dodged a bolt of lightning from above.

"Oh, and older you taught older me some magic tricks," said Hannah. "Surprise. So don't teach me anything like that, okay?"

They darted through and around the horror show in the courtyard toward the gates as quick as possible, behind them the muffled shouts of Vannah were still inside the castle but catching up. "What now?" Clamored Merlyn.

"Now, you need to make those big metal gates go KABOOM." Said Hannah.

"And then what?" He asked.

"We jump."

"Oh, hell no."

"Damn right," said Hannah. "We jump, you toss the coin, make a wish, and we go home."

"You are insane!" He shouted.

"Don't be so surprised, I've had a good teacher for the past 24 hours."

Merlyn, leaning low and still in a full sprint snatched the bone wands from his back pocket, and with one in each hand pointed them at the gate and shouted, **"ANNIHILARE!"** The concussive blast tore the giant metal doors off of their hinges like tissue paper and tossed them into the sky. With only a dozen yards to go he returned the drumsticks to the ass of his pants and snatched the metal coin for the gateway from the front pocket. As they approached the edge Hannah felt for Merlyn's empty hand and held on to it as tight as she could; then he flipped the coin and said the magic words, as they jumped from the floating castle it stopped a hundred feet below them in midair, started spinning, and a cone shaped vortex of light erupted from within. An aurora of colors crackled and the nightmare fairytale world dissolved around them as Hannah and Merlyn passed through the portal. Sensations stretched, moments became an infinite forever, the wizard felt her arms around him, her lips to his; he was happy, he was safe, and they would both be all right.

Chapter 12: Growing Up Is Hard To Do

All throughout downtown Serenity building walls crumbled and dozens of passers by died from falling debris, while hundreds more remained trapped in their collapsed edifices, now half sunk into the ground. Two entire city blocks had fallen as a result of the battle below the streets. Half a dozen blocks away from the epicenter; Kiran, Cassie, and Zeke stood in a cul-de-sac watching the smoke rise from burnt zombies while an eight foot tall behemoth holding an automatic rifle came towards them.

Frankenstein's Monster stepped over the pavement covered with charred zombie bones, snapping them apart and crunching them into little pieces as his boots fell, ash carried on the breeze and the smell of dead flesh hung heavy in the air. Kiran created an orb of fire in her hand and threw it at the monster, like a fastball it streaked through the air at him, until Sarah Harrison stepped into sight and swatted it down with her warhammer.

"Ms. Harrison?" Said Kiran.

"For cripes sake, Kiran, you've been calling me Sarah since you and Hannah were in first grade. Or at least Hannah's mom. Don't stop now." Kiran and Cassie both ran up to Sarah and wrapped their arms around her.

"Oh my God," said Cassie. "We are so glad to see you. The city's gone mad."

"Yeah, it does look like a season finale of the Walking Dead up here." Sarah looked around and then turned back to Kiran, "Where's Hannah and the wizard?" She paused. "And why do you have Johnny Storm's superpowers all of a sudden?"

"All that might take a while to explain."

"Just give me the Wikipedia summary."

"Okay, first the last. Hannah turned into a vamp last night after fighting zombies, she bit me, almost killed me, Merlyn took us back to his observatory where he did a kind of vampire exorcism on her, banishing her fangy half, at least temporarily. Meanwhile, he gave me a universal donation of wizard blood, his blood, to heal me real fast, and now I can Human Torch the hell out of things."

"Aspect of the wizard." Said Sarah.

"What?" Said Kiran.

"That's what it's called, aspect of the wizard or witch. When you gain abilities from the blood of one of the witch-breed. You got lucky, most would rather let you die than share a piece of their power with you." She paused. "But there's a price."

"I know," said Kiran. "I die young."

"We'll figure something out, I promise that it won't come to that."

"She said the same, don't worry, I trust both of you. It'll get sorted out. Zombie apocalypse to deal with first though." Kiran looked over at the monster, concerned. "Um, Han also said you went underground, what happened?"

"We failed, the bad guys blew up the lost city. Frank here teleported us out with a charm he'd been saving for a special 'oh god, we're all going to die' occasion." Sarah slapped her monstrous friend on the shoulder. "Okay then. Now where's Hannah?"

"Transdimensional walkabout." Said Kiran.

"You're kidding me."

"Nope. Ol' wacky mojo sensei decided she needed to learn something in the universe next door so he flipped a magic coin on the floor and they both jumped down into the rabbit hole. Said they'd be back pronto, something about time moving different there, y'know, like in that episode on every science fiction show ever, but so far they haven't shown back up. They might be back at the observatory but Hannah isn't answering her cell so I doubt it."

"Merlyn fucking Morningstar." Said Sarah. "Every time he shows up things go to hell. Damn it!"

"Huntress?" Said The Monster.

"I'm fine," she said. "Can't worry about that now anyway, we need to go. You take the lead, Colonel, I'll cover our backs." Sarah hadn't realized it but they were all staring at her companion. "Everyone, this is Colonel Karl Hesse, the legendary Monster of Frankenstein, and one of the greatest heroes this world has ever seen."

The monster straightened his back and dusted himself off a bit. "She exaggerates."

"Bee tee double you," said Sarah. "He's totally blushing right now, you just can't see it cause he's dead and all green and gray."

"It's a somber shade," he said. "But it speaks volumes about character."

"Okey doke, that's enough getting to know you," said Sarah. "Let's go!"

Kiran didn't budge. "We're not leaving, we can't just leave Matt behind. I have to go back to find him."

"I'm sorry, miss, we cannot stay here." Said the monster. "An army of the dead being controlled by chemical warlocks is headed this way, unless we leave right now we may all be killed."

"Take the others, I'm not leaving," said Kiran.

"The hell you aren't," said Sarah. "Letting both of you get killed doesn't solve anything, learn to run away and fight later. If Matt's alive we'll find him and help him, if he isn't, then there's nothing we can do." She grabbed Kiran by the arm and pulled her away. "Move!"

The band of friends ran south, away from most of the devastation downtown and the approaching sounds of the zombie mob, they turned down a block of halfway fallen old stone office buildings that had survived the quake, and ran smack dab into the largest congregation of chemical warlocks and dead lackeys that they had seen yet. At the end of the street a man dressed in a white lab coat with blood splattered all over it fiddled and finagled with the controls to a machine the size of Kubrick's obelisk, his voice boomed out over the crowd. "Hallo, mein Sohn! So glad you survived, I wouldn't want you to miss what happens next!"

Hannah The Huntress

*****

Hannah and Merlyn teleported right into the middle of a herd of zombies attacking a city bus full of commuters, the doors and windows were shut but the dead piled on, hundreds of the hungry creatures, pressing and banging against the glass, attempting to get in. Hannah reacted immediately, drew her swords and cut through the mob to make a path away from them; she sliced and diced, hacked and slashed, rendered limb from bloody limb, until she and Merlyn escaped the throng of dead things.

"Jesus fucking Christ!" Hannah exclaimed. "I thought we were teleporting back to the observatory, not into the third act of a George Romero movie!"

"That's where we should have ended up, someone or something pulled us here, into all of this."

Hannah looked around at the devastation around her; the crumbled buildings, the torn apart bodies scattered all over, the bus about to be broken into, and the army of zombies headed in their direction from the other end of the street. "The hell is going on? Those are chemical warlocks leading those things."

"Son of a bitch." Said Merlyn. A half dozen of the drug fueled magic wielders walked in front of the scores of zombies coming their way, they pointed and ordered the creatures to break off at intervals, to go down side streets and alleys, to find any victims that may have been hiding.

"As soon as they get inside, the zombies are going to tear apart the people on that bus." Said Hannah. "You go stall the ones coming this way and I'll help these folks, I'll help you when I get everyone clear."

Roving gangs of zombies with their warlock handlers roamed the streets of Serenity, so Merlyn walked up the block and picked a fight with one of them. A warlock without any hair wearing a Van Halen t-shirt threw a bolt of blue lightning at him, the wizard spun one of his drumsticks in the air, collecting the electricity, and hurled it right back at the bad guys. The center of their gathering exploded like they'd been hit with a mortar shell. He dragged his drumsticks across the surface of the street, lighting them like matches, tossing the fireballs at the zombies, and once he reached the crowd he stopped being subtle. Without flinching, Merlyn used the Bonham wands like a pair of revolvers; point and shoot, point and shoot, bursting zombie heads in quick succession, their gore soaking the street up to his ankles. For five minutes he fought, and at the end, all of his enemies laid dead (again) at his feet. Three of the chemical warlocks escaped but Merlyn did not follow, instead he turned back and ran to Hannah as she was finishing helping the passengers off of the bus, her zombies long since beaten.

"What took you so long?" She asked.

"Hey, my lot were considerably larger, and meaner…and never you mind why it took so long."

"Aw, well if they were meaner, then good job, you." Hannah spread her arms wide and gestured at all of the destruction. "Now what was that you said, very confidently I might add, about not worrying about the passing of time when we went on our little OZ excursion?" Said Hannah.

"I didn't think your mom would destroy the whole damn city while we were gone," said Merlyn. "And something tampered with my magic, made us arrive a couple of hours later than we should have."

"Doc Frankenstein maybe? I'm guessing he really doesn't want you screwing up whatever he has planned." Said Hannah. "And why are you automatically blaming my mom?"

"I sense her nearby."

"Not what a girl dreams about hearing from her boyfriend. Creepy much?"

"Not like that. Usually I can't, but she's in a fight right now, and she has Doombringer with her. Same immortal blacksmith made your swords, I'm attuned to all of them."

"Handy trick. Where is she?"

"South."

"Let's go."

As they rounded the next block they ran into another pack of zombies, this time without any warlocks at the head. Strays.

"Not too many, this should be easy." Hannah drove the Dragon Blade through the skull of the nearest dead guy. "Oh, fuck."

181

"Problem?" Said Merlyn.

"My sword's stuck," said Hannah, "in his head."

"Put your foot on his knee and pull!"

"It's not working, it's really in there!"

"Wiggle it from side to side a little." The wizard could barely contain his laughter as he took care of the rest of the zombies.

"God damn it, Merlyn! Would you stop screwing around and help me already."

Merlyn pointed one of his drumsticks at the zombie's head and fired a streak of green light, detonating it like a watermelon at a Galagher show. "Happy?" He said.

"Ecstatic." She flicked a chunk of brains off of her sword. "Ready to go find more dead guys to make deader?"

"Would love to. Lead the way, pretty girl."

Kiran burned the zombies as fast as possible, Cassie and Zeke bashed as many of their brains in as they could, but it wasn't enough, they seemed endless. Meanwhile, the huntress and the monster charged directly into the mass of creatures, her with Doombringer, and him with both battleaxe and broadsword in hand, they were overwhelmed by sheer numbers. Hannah and Merlyn walked around the corner just as everything went to hell.

Frankenstein's Monster paid little attention to the fighting around him, he destroyed everything and everyone in his path as he made his way to the mad doctor standing beside his machine. Even Samuel, now in his human form, slithered off out of sight. "Doctor, it is time for the long strife between us to come to an end."

The doctor breathed deep as the energy from the machine filled him with more power than he could have ever hoped for. "Yes, child, it is." Screaming, he attacked the seven foot tall monster with his bare hands, they crackled with dark energy, the two of them collided like giants in battle, neither giving ground, the only outcome, death.

Hannah found her way through the crowd of creatures to her mother, her wizard right behind her. "Mom!"

"Oh my God, Hannah!" Amidst the carnage, Sarah embraced her daughter. "Are you okay?"

Hannah hugged her back as hard as she could. "Yeah, mom. Would have been nice knowing that dad was a vampire though, that was an unpleasant surprise."

"I am so so sorry," said Sarah. "After all of this is over, I'll tell you everything."

"If we survive."

"Please, this is nothing, it's only a minor zombie apocalypse. I bet we'll even make it home in time to make fun of those silly people on those singing shows you like."

"Hey now, some of those folks are really talented, it's only the first round that's painful."

The conversation next to him droned off as the wizard looked over at the large mechanism standing on the sidewalk, he recognized it from his earlier fight with Doctor Frankenstein. "The machine!" Yelled Merlyn. "It's collecting the psychic terror from all of these deaths and channeling it as raw magic into the doctor. We have to destroy it."

With bash and smash and growl and howl the old monster seized his creator by the throat and shoulder, and began to tear him apart. His fingers broke through the flesh and collarbone and ripping the muscle down to the chest, he dug around the torso's meat and fat, and grasping the heart he ignored the doctor's screams as he pulled the still beating organ out through his shattered ribcage and threw it onto the ground.

A thousand angry zombies broke free from their warlock handlers, their master dead, no longer being controled. They were in a frenzy, tearing everything apart around them, even each other, only an insatiable hunger remained to dominate their wills.

"There isn't time." Sarah looked at Merlyn and Colonel Hesse. "We need an escape route, fast. These things are about to overwhelm us."

Amongst the commotion, Cassie had sidled up next to Sarah, she put her hand on her shoulder and whispered in her ear, "Do you remember the sixth of December?"

"You." Said Sarah.

"Now!" Screamed the witch. A pair of iron manacles appeared in Zeke's hands as he slapped them onto Merlyn's wrists. The wizard looked down in dismay, cut off from his power, as good as mortal. The football player pushed him over while the zombies and warlocks attacked everyone they could find. And then the world went insane. Cassie grabbed

Sarah's head from behind with both hands and snapped her neck in one fluid motion. Her body hit the ground, lifeless and silent, kicking up dust from all of the destruction, her head twisted to an unnatural angle. Cassie stepped over the corpse, smiling, daring Hannah to do something. Her scream was deafening as she ran to her mother lying on the ground, she knelt to shake her, nothing.

Rising to face her friend, Hannah pulled both of the swords from her scabbard, the Dragon Blade and the Phoenix Sword burst into flame as she swung them at her head. She wasn't fast enough. The witch was almost unrecognizable from the person she had been a moment ago; she was thinner and her parchment skin was stretched taut against her bones, her eyes were black and cavernous with only pinpricks of orange light peeking out of the hollows, the wind and the electricity in the air had cut her clothes to near ribbons and her sapphire blue hair whipped around her like a storm. She was also floating several inches above the ground. As the swords came at her in a sideways arc she held out the palm of her hand and stopped them, and then with a subtle gesture ripped them out of Hannah's hands, sending them flying across the street into the rubble of a collapsed building, the former site of a very nice Applebee's. Hannah didn't miss a beat, she picked up her mom's warhammer from the ground and struck Cassie in the midsection with it, like a baseball player swinging for a home run, she flew up into the air, smashing through a sign advertising shitty beer and into the top floor of one of the only buildings on the block still standing. The witch blew the side of the edifice away and leaped back down to where she had been standing.

"You'll have to do a lot better than that if you want to beat me. You're not the only one with superpowers and witty banter any more." Hannah looked over at Merlyn lying on the ground, struggling with his bonds. "Like that?" Said Cassie. "The legendary Merlyn Morningstar, undone by a little iron."

"What did you do?"

"He didn't tell you, did he? His mother is one of the Fae, iron is one of their weaknesses, hit them with it and it hurts, bind them with it and they lose their power. Not surprising, really, he always was a liar and a cheat. Not direct lies, mind you, but lies of omission, the dangerous kinds, the truths that hurt the intended."

"Or, maybe he just didn't want psycho nut jobs playing bondage and taking away his powers. It's all about perspective, Cassie, and yours is fucked right now." Hannah swung Doombringer at the witch, nearly taking her face off. For a moment it looked like the good guys might have a chance, and then it happened, the villain batted the warhammer away like it was a toy and slammed the hero to ground, collapsing the pavement around her into pieces.

The wizard watched in horror. Zeke stood next to Merlyn, staring off in the distance, dazed and confused, expressionless; Kiran walked right up to him and decked him, knocking him out in one punch, he folded onto the pavement like a rag doll. "Holy shit," said Merlyn. She tried to get the manacles off of him but to no avail. "Don't bother, they're mystical, only a special key can get these off. Take care of Zeke, get him out of here, he was enchanted, wasn't his fault."

"How am I supposed to do that? He's a little heavier than I am."

"My blood, you have access to elemental forces now, fire isn't your only trick. Use the air around us, lift him out of here." Kiran held both of her shaking hands out towards Zeke, slow and steady, he started to float a couple of feet above the ground. "Now go!" Yelled the wizard.

"We'll be back," said Kiran. "I promise." Merlyn nodded.

The fight between Hannah and Cassie wasn't going well, the witch had her pinned to the ground and was hitting her repeatedly with her bloody fists. His wrists chained together and bound in iron manacles, the wizard stumbled to his feet, ran straight at Cassie, raised his arms and slammed her in the back of the head as he tackled her to the pavement. "Monster!" Yelled Merlyn. "Get her the hell out of here!" A group of mystical minions pulled him off of Cassie and threw him aside, then attacked, he writhed on the ground as the chemical warlocks took turns hitting him with spell after spell.

Frankenstein's Monster picked Hannah off of the pavement, and before leaving grabbed the enchanted warhammer, throwing it into the bag of weapons hanging from his side. He ran down the street, his enormous strides covering great distance in little time, finally he caught up with Kiran and Zeke. She was sitting on a curb, exhausted, catching her breath, the boy passed out beside her. "Allow me," said The Monster. With Hannah still in his arms, he picked up the boy and tossed him over his shoulder. "Can you walk?"

"Kiran looked up at him, tears in her eyes. "I can sure the hell walk out of here."

*****

The Valkyrie and the soldier stared down at their daughter's lifeless body, they held each other close and they cried for the woman they had never been allowed to know. Around them the entire world came to a halt; the clocks did not tick, the wind did not stir, no living creature moved at all. They were between moments, where thought and action did not exist for mortals.

"We should have done more," said the soldier.

"That isn't the way of things, my love, we could not." They knelt next to Sarah's body, the soldier closed her eyes as the Valkyrie ran her hand through her daughter's hair, and then she lifted her up into her arms. "We must go."

The soldier smiled at his eternal love. "I'm staying behind," he said.

"You cannot," she said.

"I am."

"They will come for you."

"Let them," he said. "This world is already wrong, we've seen it, thing's aren't the way they should be. We failed our daughter, and I won't abandon our granddaughter now to misery and death, she'll need allies in the days ahead."

"If that is your choice then I will not argue, but be prepared, the Guardians of Valhalla will not rest until you are reclaimed. I will do what I can to stall them but it will not be enough. And there are far worse fates than death. Be ever vigilant."

"I understand the cost, and it's one that I'll gladly pay to watch over Hannah."

"Forever the hero," said the Valkyrie. "Sarah and I will wait for you at the end."

The sound of the wind crept up, signaling that linear time was once again about to resume, the soldier kissed his daughter's forehead and then his wife's lips. The Valkyrie looked up, her dark wings spread out, over a dozen feet from tit to tip, moving silently against the air as she started to rise towards the sky. A break in the clouds opened far above as the two of them soared through a ray of sunshine that touched the earth.

For a moment the soldier glowered at the frozen witch who had murdered his daughter, he put his hand on her throat and squeezed. "It would be so easy," he said. "But that isn't what's supposed to happen. You're someone else's problem." Time quickened, slowly at first and then faster, the breeze in the air, the smell of rain in the distance, the blink of an eye; he eased away as everything moved again, back to the shadows of a nearby alley where he disappeared into the darkness.

*****

Villains all around hooted and hollered as the heroes ran away, the zombies swayed and lurked about while the chemical warlocks cast dark magic in celebration; a purple cartoon dinosaur made of light demolished a storefront, the post office on the corner was frozen over by three spellbinders working in unison, and a flesh golem conjured together from the contents of a butcher shop chased a women in a red hat with a yellow feather in it into a pack of hyenas standing upright on their hind legs. They ate her. Meanwhile, the wicked witch watched and waited, gleeful to witness such carnage.

Cassie kicked the left side of Doctor Frankenstein's gutted corpse, the side without a head. "Too bad," she said. "He was a faithful retainer."

"You're not going to resurrect him?" Asked Samuel.

"I don't think so. He served his purpose, and we all know what they say about too many cooks spoiling the broth."

"Good," replied Samuel with a wicked smile.

"Thought you might approve, he didn't treat you very well, did he?" she said.

Samuel leaned on a makeshift cane, a femur taken from a pile of bones discarded after a group of zombies finished their meal. "No. He never appreciated me, never rewarded me, two centuries and he wouldn't fulfill his promise."

"I am so sorry, my friend, but now you need not worry. You will be freed from your demon. Soon." She said. "Now. Who do you serve?"

The crippled man inclined his head. "You, mistress. Only you now."

"Glad to hear it," she said. The witch clapped her hands together, making a louder than normal bang. "We have things to do and not a lot of time, I just murdered that girl's mom and stole her boyfriend, she may have run away for now but in a little while she's going to come gunning for my pretty ass. SO…let's get this carnival of freaks on the road!"

"What do you require of me?" Asked Samuel.

"Your other half," said Cassie. "I know it is a burden, faithful one, but the warlocks need their overseer to reign them in and they in turn with the zombies. Think of it like the supernatural world's circle of fear, with me on top, and you beneath me." She twisted her fingers through his hair. "Mmm…now doesn't that sound nice? Change, and let them cower before you."

"As you wish." The transformation was almost instantaneous this time, Samuel let go of the bone cane and by the time it hit the pavement the Snake Man had taken his place.

"Gather my armies to me," said Cassie. "It's time for us to leave this place." As his human self had just done, the Snake Man inclined his head in obedience, he left her side, and ran snarling and hissing into the nearest crowd of zombies.

Pandemonium reigned, the citizens of Serenity ran for their lives from the monsters stalking their streets, flames gutted building after building, those fallen and those still standing, and all throughout, pleas for mercy pierced the air. "Oh, I almost forgot." Cassie motioned in a come hither way to the rubble across the street. **"LEMMAS EMOS."** Rustling came from the fallen rubble as Hannah's Chinese butterfly swords flew into the air and into Cassie's outstretched hands. "Marvelous," she said. Light from the proximate fires glinted off of the blades, Cassie heard their comforting song inside of her mind. "So that was your plan," she looked down at the unconscious wizard. "Supernatural Soma. Keep little Hannah happy and the big bad vampire within at bay." She sliced his shirtsleeve and cut his right forearm open with the tip of the Phoenix Sword, eliciting a groan from his comatose bag of bones. "We'll just have to see how she holds up when the fighting starts, you know, with no swords, and an enchanted Viking warhammer in her possession that craves bloodshed. Too bad she picked that up, huh? Oops. Silly me."

"Mistresssss," said the snake man. "They are circling in clossssser, as you commanded."

Cassie tucked the swords into her belt. "Good. Be so kind and carry the wizard over next to the great machine, I'd hate for my favorite new playthings to get separated." He picked up Merlyn, threw him over his scaly shoulder, and went over by the big ol' Jack Kirby nightmare looking contraption. "Everyone scooch in real close now! Wouldn't want to lose anyone on the way there!" The witch pointed to the machine and a bolt of mystical energy shot out from it to her fingertips, then with the same hand she reached to the sky and shouted, **"MAS PAREI STO MATI TOU THEOU!"** Wind howled, thunder cracked, the ground shook, a heavy dark fog appeared, and by the time it dissipated the witch and her army of monsters had disappeared from sight.

*****

The Harrison home felt warm and safe as Frankenstein's Monster carried Hannah inside and set her down on the couch, for a man so large it was astonishing how gentle Karl Hesse could be. Her sleep was erratic, full of nightmares and movement, spurred on by the last spell the witch hit her with.

"Will she be all right?" Asked Kiran

"I believe so," said the monster. "I've seen magic like this before, the affects are strong but brief, the old German fairy tales are replete with them." Zeke was still slung over his shoulder and starting to come around, he placed the boy down onto a big comfy chair that sat in the corner of the room by a bookcase and a tall reading lamp.

"The hell happened to me?" He said rubbing his jaw. "Feels like somebody decked me."

"Sorry about that," said Kiran. "To be fair, you kinda had it coming. What do you remember?"

"Oh Christ." Zeke shook his head, "All of it, I think. It was like watching myself from the other end of a tunnel, I wanted to stop, but I couldn't."

"It's okay," she said. "Wasn't your fault." Kiran leaned over the side of the chair and gave him a hug. "None of us could have expected Cassie to turn on us."

A glass bowl, jade green with small flowers painted on it smashed into the far wall. "The hell we couldn't," said Hannah, sitting up on the couch, the bowl's lid had come off, she sat it on the coffee table while eyeing the pieces on the floor. "We've been friends for all of our damn lives, we should have seen that something was wrong."

"It doesn't make any sense, I don't understand how Cassie could do those things." Said Kiran.

"I doubt if that was your friend," said the monster.

"What do you mean?" Asked Hannah.

"Appearances don't mean very much when it comes to the dark corners of this world and the creatures that inhabit it. When you've been around as long as I have you start to develop a feel for these things."

"Like Spidey sense," said Hannah.

Colonel Hesse raised an eyebrow and continued. "Er, yes, I suppose so." He looked pensive. "And what I saw doesn't add up, the magicks wielded by that witch were far more than what any novice teenager should have been able to accomplish."

"All right, if not her then who?"

"I do not know, but whoever it is, possesses enough raw power and mystical ability that they were able to turn my creator into a mere lackey. In over two hundred years, Victor Frankenstein never served anything or anyone but his own corrupt ambitions, however she subjugated him and with whatever she promised him to comply, we must be wary. The only thing the mad doctor ever worshipped was death, whoever she is, we can be certain that her might is considerable."

"Great," said Hannah. "Then either our friend is an unstoppable evil bitch thing, just plain crazy powerful or something really bad's happened to the real Cassie. Well, no matter which shit sandwich we choose we have to do something and we have to do it fast." Doombringer was leaning against the corner next to the couch, she grabbed it and held it out in front of her, examining the duality of the warhammer and the axe, immediately the drums of war began to beat inside her mind. "Because either way, the Cassie running around out there murdered my mom, took my boyfriend, and leveled part of the city while killing who knows how many people. I'm going to make her answer for that."

"Don't forget saving the world." Said Kiran.

"Yeah, that too." Said Hannah.

With the drapes open they watched as an amber light pulsed from the top of the hill above the observatory, it quickened, faster and faster until it exploded like fireworks on the Fourth of July. The golden light burst out from the high center and then arced down on equal sides, solidifying into a dome covering the buildings and the land around them, obfuscating the observatory within.

"Huh, least she made that simple, we won't have to look for her," said Hannah. "Cassie and her new friends are at the observatory."

"The witch has erected an Electrum Shield, it will be difficult to penetrate."

Kiran lifted an eyebrow, "There is so much double entendre wrong with what you just said." Everyone ignored her, too tired to laugh or smile. "Sorry, guys. Just my typical nerves working overtime. Please continue."

"Looks like an insect trapped in amber." Said Hannah.

"That's exactly what it is," said the monster. "And coursing with a mystical current."

"Electricity?"

"Essentially, most magicks have a basis in science, they just twist the details to serve other purposes."

"Okay, league, I'm tired of just reacting to bad thing after bad thing as they hit us, and I'm tired of asking questions when the answers all suck," said Hannah. "It's time for all of us to act, to make our own answers, it's time to save the city before more people die, and it's time for us to send this uber she-witch back to whatever second rate hell she crawled out of."

"She-witch?" Asked Kiran. "You mean just plain old witch?"

"Shut up, you." Replied Hannah.

"So what's the plan? Said Zeke.

"No plan," said Hannah. "We storm the castle and kill the evil bitch of the west."

"Really?" Asked Kiran.

"Well, no, I actually have kind of a plan, one that I need all of your help with." Hannah turned to the giant next to her and put her hand on his arm. "Colonel Hesse, you've already done so much for all of us, and before that for my mom, I feel hesitant asking you for anything else, but we…I could really use your help with what comes next."

Frankenstein's noble monster drew himself up to his full height, pulled his massive longsword from its scabbard and said, "With the doctor destroyed my tether to this world is fading, even now I can feel the approaching end to my long existence. But for whatever time I have left on the mortal plane I pledge my sword to you, Huntress. It is my honor to serve at your side in the battle against the darkness."

"Thank you," said Hannah. "Mom always said you were amazing, turns out that didn't even come close to describing just how awesome you are. Although you might want to rethink everything after you hear what I have to say."

"Oh crap," said Kiran. "She's got that look, like when cute jackets are on sale. This can't be good."

Hannah ignored her flippant friend. "The weather forecast calls for some serious shit to happen tonight. We're going to use that to our advantage and then we're going to kick every single one of their evil asses."

"What do you want me to do?" Asked Zeke. He'd been quiet and sitting with his head down, his expression distant and removed from everything and everyone, but now he stood up from the couch and met Hannah's eyes with his own, determined. "I don't know what the hell happened to Cassie, or how she got like this, or if that's even her, but I promise I'll do whatever it takes to stop that witch."

"No, you're not going to fight Cassie, I won't ask you to do that. Besides, as far as we know the whammy she laid on you could still be working and you'd turn on us in the middle of the fight. None of us can be certain." Zeke looked dejected. "It's not your fault, we all know that. Find Matt," she said. "I refuse to let that witch force us to abandon our friend to die. Concentrate on searching around that coffee shop, he has to be nearby somewhere, and alive, he's there somewhere, he just has to be."

"Okay, General Sassy Vixen, how bout me?"

"Kiran, I'm going to need you to kill an army of zombies while Frank and I handle the warlocks and the uber-witch."

"Cool."

"Really? No questions, no lingering self doubt?"

"Nope, I'm feeling all hyped up on elemental wizard powers and pretty damn victorious. Plus! You have just the outfit for that, which I am going to borrow."

"Oh God, what do you want?"

"Your dark red leather pants and that black Fulci Zombie baby tee you got at the mall last weekend. Oh, and those cute black boots you bought on sale at that place near the other place a few weeks ago."

"No way! Not the boots, those are perfect and almost broken in, your weird feet will do weird things to them."

"My weird feet?" Said Kiran. "Um, Big Foot much, Han?"

"What? I have cute toes." Kiran gave Hannah a 'that's BS and you know it look.' "Okay, fine, deal, but I want 'em back"

"No promises. Evildoers have no respect for other people's property, these boots could go missing at any time. Whisked away right in the heat of battle!"

"Yeah, and right into your overflowing shoe closet."

"I like to think of it as a shoe cave, where some of them hibernate through the passage of the seasons and emerge rested and eager to be worn."

Frankenstein's Monster cleared his throat, everyone turned their heads. "Sorry. If the shoe talk had continued for much longer I would have been compelled to switch sides."

"No evil shoe divas in your past?" Asked Hannah.

"Only one, during the Siege of St. Petersburg, although they were calling it Leningrad back in those days. A Russian vampire of the aristocracy who had escaped the October Revolution and exacted her revenge by collecting the shoes of her Communist victims...while their feet were still in them."

"Gross," said Kiran. "What Happened?"

"I snuck into the city, chopped off her head, burned her corpse, and snuck out again."

"Good to know," said Hannah. "Shelving the shoe talk."

"Now, what do you require of me," said the monster.

"Colonel Hesse," said Hannah. "Think you could survive a lightning strike."

A surprising and toothy grin lit up the Monster of Frankenstein's face. "Ja, it is as easy as being born again, mein freund."

"Then everyone get ready. When the clock strikes midnight, we're going to show Cassie or whoever the fuck that is, that she just messed with the wrong League of Monster Fighting Badasses."

Chapter 13: Convergence

Lightning tore the sky asunder, thunder shook the ground, and the wind howled as Frankenstein's Monster marched up the hill to the observatory. The light flickered and flashed, casting deep shadows from the buildings ahead down the road, they illuminated the monster, revealing the myth garbed in Prussian blue. He wore his old cavalry jacket over his black fatigues; dark blue with polished gold buttons and saffron laces, four rows across the breast and stomach, and likewise hued cuffs, medals and high collar insignia. In his right hand he hefted his trusted battle axe as it rested on his shoulder, the reflection from the storm highlighted the scene wrought into the two half moon blades, a forest on one side and on the other a home resting on the slopes of a mountain beside a gentle stream. Across his back was his mighty broad sword waiting to be drawn, its hilt shining bright despite the darkness, he carried a large bag of firearms in his left hand, and slung over that shoulder was a long black cylindrical tube, the kind architects use to carry plans.

Kneeling before the amber opaque dome covering the hilltop, Colonel Hesse touched its surface, he felt the electric hum, and in his mind heard the song that was sung to cast such a spell. "Beautiful," he whispered. Vague shapes moved back and forth on the other side, the army of the witch; perhaps a thousand zombies, dozens of chemical warlocks, and the boss of bosses at the end of the game, a dark sorceress imbued with so much raw power that she dared to become a new goddess for the world to worship and fear. However, The Monster of Frankenstein had killed a god or two in his day, so he set about on his task, ready to play his part in the unfolding drama; he opened the cylindrical tube he carried and withdrew the Franklin lightning rod, then raised it high above him, its base touching the mystical barrier, and he waited for the call.

The Silver Surfer was waiting at the bottom of the hill, engine purring, Kiran sat in the driver's seat staring straight ahead and tapping the steering wheel with her fingers, Hannah knelt on top of the car's roof. She grabbed her phone out of her jacket pocket and hit send, Frankenstein's Monster picked up. "Get ready, Colonel, we're on our way." After lowering a pair of welding goggles over her eyes she banged on the metal beneath her feet and shouted, "HIT IT!"

Kiran slammed the car into gear and punched the accelerator, the Karman Ghia roared up the narrow road to the top of the hill. With the warhammer in her right hand, Hannah held tight to the seem between the windshield and the metal roof with her left as she crouched like a surfer on a board, *this is fitting,* she thought. Her dark hair waving behind her and her black jacket whipping in the wind, she screamed into the darkness ahead, daring it to do its worst. And then the AC/DC started to wail out of the window beneath her, *I was caught, In the middle of a railroad track. (Thunder) I looked round, And I knew there was no turning back...*

Another bolt flashed in the heavens, whiting out the sky, the silhouette of Frankenstein's Monster glowed green and blue against the dark background of the observatory as the lighting struck him and the metal conductor he held against the shield. Kiran crested over the hilltop fifty yards away, shifted down, stomped on the brakes and turned the Silver Surfer into a sideways slide, Hannah launched herself high into the air and came down swinging the power forged warhammer with all of her supernatural strength.

You've been...

THUNDERSTRUCK!

Devastation rang out, the impact alongside the lightning strike created a mystical explosion that lit up the entire countryside, she and Doombringer shattered the enchantment covering the observatory and the witch's army, an electric cascade rained down with her to the ground, the shield fell like burning scraps of paper caught on the breeze.

Before she could stand, three chemical warlocks attacked Hannah; they lashed her hands and feet together with barbed wire, lifted her body several inches off of the ground, and hung her upside down. One of the warlocks, a man with filthy long hair, a scraggly beard and broken teeth, expelled a swarm of wasps from his mouth, they circled and crisscrossed around Hannah, forming a makeshift cage.

A line of fire shot through the air seeking out the wasps and turned them to ash, Colonel Hesse and Kiran following right behind it. Thrown from twenty yards away and spinning through the air, his broadsword struck swift and true, straight through the heart of the warlock with the broken teeth, and beside him the other two were dispatched as the monster caught their necks in mid stride and snapped them with ease in each of his giant hands. Hannah dropped to the ground, burst free of her barbed shackles, and picked up Doombringer from where it had landed a couple of feet away.

"Thanks, guys," she said.

"Why aren't the zombies attacking us?" Asked Kiran. "They're all just standing around over next to the observatory."

"They're protecting Super-Cassie while she works some evil mojo with that machine. We need to get over there and smash it to pieces before she has a chance to use it and becomes even evil-er."

"Then what?"

"Then I work out some of my anger issues. On her face." All three of them were quickly surrounded by glass eyed chemical warlocks crackling with temporary magicks and high as proverbial kites. "Okay, hot stuff, you take the army of dead guys in the back, we'll take care of all of the Orange is the new Azkaban wannabes. My dear Colonel, let's clear a path for the lady."

"Ah, fraulein, I thought you'd never ask." The Monster wielded both battleaxe and broadsword as he carved a hole into the mass of evil doers ahead of him, blood and guts spilled and sprayed everywhere while he hacked through flesh with reckless abandon, an afterlife of rage let loose against his foes.

Hannah somersaulted above the crowd and crashed into a warlock floating there who had partially morphed into a human sized plucked chicken, beak and all. She knocked him out with a left hook and drove him into another group of magic casters attempting to stop Kiran with an animated walking and talking willow tree. As she landed on top of them, breaking up their chanting circle, she looked over her should and watched as her friend directed a fireball into the trunk of the tree, causing it to explode in front of her in a hail of smoldering kindling.

Another dozen chemical warlocks converged on Hannah and Kiran, cutting them off from the zombie army protecting Cassie and the great machine. Out of the corner of Hannah's eye she saw The Monster charge at the surrounding warlocks from the left side, his bladed weapons were sheathed and he was unloading two uzis into them. Two were able to put up shields, most of the others were ripped apart by the torrent of bullets. With a downwards blow Hannah smashed in the skull of one of the survivors on the ground, then decapitated a second with the axe half of the warhammer as she spun sideways to her right. Colonel Hesse threw the uzis back into his bag of weapons that was hanging to his side, drew a Desert Eagle handgun from his shoulder holster and finished off the rest of the wounded chemical warlocks with single shots.

The hillside in front of the observatory was clear. "You're up," said Hannah pointing to the mass of slobbering zombies between them and their goal.

"Fucking hell," said Kiran as she stared at the headless body a couple of feet away. "What did you do? Those were still people, not mindless monsters."

"Whatever I have to." Said Hannah."

"I know you're hurting and upset, but your mom would not want this." Said Kiran. "Hell, I don't want you to do this." She lowered her voice and motioned at Frankenstein's Monster. "Him, I expect it from, but you're not some mad scientist's messed up experiment. You're not a killer."

"Yes. I am." Said Hannah, she stated it with finality and a cool look in her eyes. "If the last day has taught me, and it should have taught you, anything, it's that I was born to be a killer." She touched her friend's arm with her bloody hand. "Sweet Kiran, we don't have time for teenage drama, today we make the hard choices that will set us down our paths for the rest of our lives. You're mad...and that's a good thing. Use that anger against the dead, show that witch what a goddess shrouded in fire looks like."

"This isn't over." Kiran turned away from her best friend and set off towards the zombies. Where she walked, her footsteps scorched the dirt and grass, she burst into flames, letting it grow like a miniature sun, the fire and heat coming off of her so hot that it distorted the air. The army of the dead descended upon her, thrashing and groaning, biting and tearing; Kiran Amanat, seventeen and angry, screamed her frustrations as loud as she could, and then proceeded to burn them all from the face of the Earth.

*****

"Merlyn, Merlyn!" Yelled Matt. "Wake the hell up, man." The wizard was bound in iron manacles and chained to the floor in the same room where he had locked up Hannah less than a day before. Two chemical warlocks remained outside the closed door, keeping watch over their prisoner. "Jesus Christ, dude, you need to get up right fucking now, it's getting apocalyptic out there."

"Please stop yelling," croaked Merlyn. Shaking his head he sat up on the floor. "Seriously, my head hurts so bad I feel like I could barf." He paused, looking at his hands. "I need to get these lovely iron bracelets off."

"Why can't you zap 'em off?"

"Because they're made of iron and I'm basically allergic to them, my mom was one of the Fae."

"Fae?"

"Fairy folk. Think Tinker Bell but bigger and scarier. You need to get me the keys."

"Dude, I can't get anything for you right now."

"Why not?" Said Merlyn. Then he realized why and raised his eyebrow like Mr. Spock on Star Trek. "And why the hell can I see through you?"

"Got hurt bad back in town, when I woke up I was like this, all see through and standing over my own body. After I found everyone else and they couldn't see or hear me I figured that I better come look for you, I mean if anyone can help, it's you. At least when you're not all locked up and weakened by your own personal Kryptonite."

"Yeah, wizards and witches are sensitive to ghosts and astral projections, you did good coming to find me. That's what you are, by the way, an astral projection, it's like a ghost but from people that are still alive. Usually they're evoked on purpose, from magic practitioners using deep meditation techniques to leave their bodies. In your case it was your spirit self's natural reaction to being harmed. You keep impressing me, kid, what takes others decades to master is second nature to you."

"I'm glad you're impressed and all but this really sucks. Am I going to be all right?"

"You should be, just have to get you back into your body before you die. Easy enough to do, I'll guide you back once all of this is over."

"Cool. Just please, don't get killed."

A cocky smile broke out on the wizard's face. "Have you met me?" He said as he laughed. "Listen, I need you to fling those keys sitting on the nightstand over to me." Said Merlyn.

"How the hell am I supposed to do that? I'm a fricken ghost, remember?"

"Exactly, and most ghosts slash astral projections have a limited form of spectral telekinesis."

"Okay, I guess…I mean I'll try," said Matt.

"There is no try, so just use the damn force already, kid."

Ghost Matt waved his hand like he was trying to slap someone. "The fuck are doing?" Said Merlyn. "They're keys, not a fart."

"Any suggestions from the locked up and weak as a kitten smartass wizard?"

"Just concentrate, use your will, be like Chevy Chase in Caddyshack, be the ball." Matt looked at him with an 'Are you fucking kidding me stare?' "Okay, whatever, be the keys in this case." He tried again, this time without moving.

The keys started to rattle, jumping up and down, jingling back and forth, and then they flew off of the nightstand right into Merlyn's outstretched hands. "Well done!" He shouted a bit too loud. Fumbling with the key to the manacles he managed to unlock himself within a few seconds as the chemical warlocks guarding him burst through the door. Merlyn stepped outside of the circle with the cross inside of it and with both hands, raised the two sentries up to the ceiling with his power, choking the life out of them.

"That's him, on the right," whispered Ghost Matt into Merlyn's ear. "That's the prick who buried me alive."

"Then it's time to even the score, possess him, and do what you need to do."

"I can do that?"

"Damn right."

"Finally! Something cool about this shitty situation."

Ghost Matt concentrated and then stepped inside of the dirty dreadlock douchebag, the villain immediately started to sweat and his eyes rolled back into his head, when he looked forward again his blue irises were gone and just the black pupil against the white remained. "This is weird," said Matt with the warlock's voice.

"Different how?" Asked Merlyn.

"Everything. It's all colder and more remote, feels even stranger than being a ghost, like the entire world's one giant fucked up Twilight Zone episode and I'm now one of the actors." Matt stepped out of the guy's body, the warlock slumped to the floor, passed out. "Had to get out of there. I don't need revenge, that isn't who I want to be. So just knock this other idiot out and let's go."

Merlyn clapped his hands next to the warlock on the left and let him collapse to the floor, unconscious. "I'm proud of you, kid, it takes guts not to give in to temptation and to kill a soon to be harmless enemy. Once the majeesh wears off those two won't be worth a damn anymore."

"So that was a test?"

"Not exactly, if you'd killed him I wouldn't have thought twice about it, wannabe Death Eater had it coming. But I'd be more cautious of you and your talents at this stage, right now I trust you like I would few others."

"Not sure whether to take that as a compliment or a warning."

"Little bit of both," said Merlyn. "Any more guards?"

"I didn't see any others on my way inside."

"Pity, I'm in a terrible mood, woulda been cathartic." He and ghost Matt left the kinky chain-me-up room and walked down the hallway to the living room and the observatory, keeping an eye out for more warlocks as they went. "I'll be damned," said Merlyn. "I think that arrogant witch only left those two behind, her mistake." Merlyn stopped in the kitchen, turned on the faucet, ducked his head under to take a big quenching drink, splashed water on his face, and drew a circle of sparkling lights in the air with his index finger. **"Quod est praeter me,"** he said. The impromptu scrying pool showed him the battle outside; Frankenstein's Monster was holding back the remaining chemical warlocks and a small group of leftover zombies while Hannah fought Cassie, distracting her as Kiran made her way over to destroy the great machine. "There isn't much time left, the witch almost has all of the power she'll need to open the gateway between worlds."

"That's bad, right?"

"Yeah, it's Apocalypse Now without the laughs."

"Gotcha, so how do we stop it? Help Kiran?"

"No, by stopping her from destroying it," said Merlyn. "How long you been haunting everyone?"

"Huh?" Said ghost Matt, confused. "Since just after Cassie murdered Hannah's mom and the rest of them fled back to her house. The hell's going on?"

"That isn't Cassie," said Merlyn. "She's only wearing her face. I couldn't sense it before because she was using some damn strong concealment spells but once she started casting I recognized the witch's magic."

"Who is she?" Asked Matt.

"Someone angry and powerful enough to flatten a big part of the continent unless we stop her." Merlyn waved his hand at the circle, bringing the image of the machine closer. "Stop Kiran, find the secret inside of that machine and bring it to either Hannah or myself."

"But you're the only one that can see and hear me," said Matt.

The wizard held up his right hand to the wispy spectre and muttered a quiet spell, like being seen with a new pair of glasses, Ghost Matt suddenly came into focus. "There, you're still just an astral projection, but the others should be able to see and talk to you now." Matt examined his hands as if they were something new and shiny. "Go! Stop her from destroying that machine!" He passed right through the living room wall and into the thick of the battle as Merlyn called after him. "I need to get some things first, be there in a few minutes!"

Merlyn opened the door to the observatory and found what he expected, nothing. The intruder wards had worked the way they were supposed to, in the event that a malicious mystical presence was detected the weapons and artifacts would disappear into a pocket dimension that exists outside of time and space, and would remain there unless recalled by the wizard of the house. Shutting the door he moved to the nearby kitchen and picked up a knife form the block on the counter, he sliced his palm open and squeezed his fist until the blood covered his whole hand, and then he placed his bloody handprint on the door. Bright light shined around the frame, and a loud crash echoed from inside as Merlyn opened the door again; his armory of supernatural weapons and artifacts had reappeared as expected. He walked over to a brown leather bound bible lying on a messy workbench with the word "auspicium" written on the bottom in gold filament and flipped it open, the wizard reached his arm into the pages, like breaking the surface of water the words rippled out from the center of contact. He withdrew a five foot tall silver and black scythe carved with Egyptian hieroglyphics.

"Father," said Merlyn as he inspected the weapon. "I need your help."

An eerie silence filled the room until it was interrupted by a quiet disembodied voice, seemingly coming from nowhere and everywhere at once. "My son. What is it that you ask of me?"

"Power to defeat my enemies." Said Merlyn. "I agree to your offer."

A frightening hush filled the room until the wizard was answered. "LET THE BARGAIN BE STRUCK!" Boomed the voice.

Sulfur and brimstone surrounded Merlyn's body as he was transformed; the wizard screamed while his soul was being burned away, gray-white wings ruptured outwards from beneath his back, six feet from fold to tip, Cimmerian horns grew a foot tall from the top of his head and curled back in on themselves, his face changed in seconds and where a beautiful young man was before, a man with cracked stone like skin, the wings of an angel, and the horns of a goat replaced him. Seething with supernatural energy, he gripped the scythe, gestured at the heavy oak door leading to the battle outside, and blew it to smithereens. With a scowl plastered across his face he stepped outside to kick a little ass.

*****

"Where is she? What did you do with my mother's body?" Shouted Hannah. She and the witch fought like dueling masters next to the entrance to the observatory, countering each other's every blow; moving, shielding and blocking as they both attempted to land the fatal stroke.

"Nothing," said the witch. "Believe it or not this is just one of those miraculous happenings you hear about on the news. Like those food items idiots find that look like Jesus."

Hannah and Cassie froze as the door to the observatory exploded outwards. "She's telling the truth, I felt the hand of divinity as Sarah's body was taken from the mortal plane. Think of it like a Jedi becoming one with the force after they die." He stopped, pulled the Celestial Twins from the witch's belt with a gesture, and caught them both one handed. "That's about all she's telling the truth about though."

"Merlyn?" Said Hannah. The glare from the electrical storm reflected off of his burnished black horns, his face looked leathery, lined, older than it had before, and his wings scraped across the surface as he walked.

"Hey, pretty lady, try not to lose these again." Merlyn threw the Chinese butterfly swords next to Hannah and slammed his reaper's scythe into the bottom of the last step outside of the observatory, the resulting shock wave threw Cassie aside before she could finish casting. "Hey witchy woman, let's tussle."

"Wizard," said Cassie as she regained her balance. "I'm not sure how you escaped, but you know what? I'm happy that you did. What's the point of becoming an all powerful goddess if you can't use your might to smite the competition?"

"I'm not a god, and neither are you, you deluded lunatic."

"Hmm…Son of Satan anyway, suppose I'll just have to settle for destroying an annoying little demi-god then. You'll make good practice for taking on the really important apocalyptic figures."

"You're not omnipotent yet lady, hell, you aren't even who you appear to be." He said. "You've been using all of us for months, sometimes from a distance and sometimes right next to us. I should have seen through it, but you're so much more powerful than you used to be. You were even able to hide you mystic signature from me, I didn't even suspect until you got me back here and let your guard down to access the machine." The wizard began to walk towards the witch, both of them gathering supernatural energies in preparation to strike at the other. "What's wrong? Afraid to show your true face, think wearing that girl's will buy you some sympathy and hesitation? Not from me, and not from them any longer." Merlyn opened his mouth wide and yelled, **"OSTENDE TE!"** From his throat a sonic boom bellowed forth, it hit counterfeit Cassie's face, causing it to become distorted and to twist inward, like a whirlpool of flesh and bone. Steam, sweat, and blood started to pour off of her skin mask as her features reset themselves to their original visage, a moment later, Allison Kosh, the Witch of Wichita, and the greatest sorceress of this era stood in front of them.

"Aunt Allie?" Said Hannah. "No, no no no no no, not you, it can't be you." Tears rolled down Hannah's face and her entire body shook from the realization that her mom's best friend, her surrogate aunt and confidante, had been the one to kill Sarah with so much callousness and disregard. "WHY?" She screamed. "Mom loved you! We both did! How could you do this?"

The witch turned her bleary face toward Hannah and regarded her with scorn. "Easily. Your mother was the fool that got rid of most of this world's ambient magicks along with all of the vampires, sentencing me and those alike, the witch-breed of this reality to a life of misery and half madness. We were all damaged because of what Sarah Harrison, the almighty Huntress did to save the world! Because of her we're nothing more than pale reflections of the marvelous beings that we should have been, deaf and blind, without purpose or salvation."

"You should have told her," said Hannah. "She would have helped you, I know she would have."

"Oh, I did," said Allison. "For years your mother and I tried to figure out a way to bring back the magic to this world, but the only answer was to open the door to Duat again, to the withered realm of old Seth. And that she would not do, not to save your father, and not to help me."

"So you murdered her in cold blood instead."

"She would have stopped me, I didn't have any other choice."

"That's nonsense, you're just like all of the other crazies who try to these stupid schemes, insane cowards too afraid to face the world as it is. So you throw a grand mal supernatural fit and the rest of us get to suffer."

The madwoman drew a frowny face in the air with the fire at the end of her fingertip, like a sparkler. "I loathe this dead universe that surrounds me," said The Witch of Wichita. "I miss the world that used to be, before all of this, this nothing, when magic coursed across the lands like the mightiest of rivers, when even the lowest among the magi were as gods walking the earth. Your dear mother took that away from me, so yes, I enjoyed finally being able to snap her miserable neck. You should thank me for making it quick, she deserved so much more suffering than that."

"Thank you? Fuck you, crazy lady."

"Tisk tisk, such course language. What would Sarah say?"

"She'd tell me to kick your bony ass," said Hannah. "Too bad you didn't kill me also, but you sure as hell tried. That

217

was you, wasn't it? You knew my dad, you're the one who caused me to vamp out last night, probably hoping that Merlyn would have to finish me off to stop me from killing everyone."

"I didn't count on the wizard saving you, then again, he always was the 'pull a rabbit out of a hat' type."

"And you took my swords and left Doombringer behind on purpose too, maybe thinking its violent nature would bring the beast out in me again, so either you'd have an ally or at least one less enemy."

"Two for two, it's unfortunate that your mom can't be here, she'd be all sorts of proud right now." Allison tossed her head back and laughed.

"Nice try, but it'll take a little more than some third rate pre social media old-lady-taunting to make me lose my cool." Hannah threw the warhammer aside and picked up the swords, the Dragon Blade and the Phoenix Sword glowed green and red in her hands, their comforting song playing in her mind. "Ah, that's so much better. Swear to God, tote around that warhammer all day and it starts to feel like non-stop Viking death metal in your head after a while."

"Sounds kinda cool to me," said Merlyn.

"Was pretty neat for an hour or two, but after breaking that wimpy shield I was ready for a little Sarah McLaughlin to soften things up. Damn, what a headache."

"ENOUGH!" Yelled the witch.

"Oh, right," said Hannah. "You've got a beat down coming. Let's get to it then." The Wizard and the Huntress rushed the witch, Hannah tightened her knuckles around the hilt of the Dragon Blade and punched her in the throat with the pommel of the sword. "Hurts when someone takes away your dreams, doesn't it? In fact, I bet you're dreaming about breathing right now."

From out of nowhere the snake man tackled Hannah, knocking her away from Allison. Without hesitation Merlyn picked the witch up, launched himself into the air and threw her into an oncoming bolt of lightning. Hannah watched from the ground as Allison shook off the sudden electrocution, steadied herself in midair, conjured a firestorm full of burning serpents and directed it at Merlyn. It was like witnessing two giants slapping the shit out of each other with the fate of the world at stake.

*****

Ghost Matt jumped out in front of Kiran just as she was about to demolish the great machine with an enormous fireball. "STOP!"

"Jesus jumping Christ," exclaimed Kiran. "Matt? The hell are you doing? I almost turned you into a ghost. What happened to you back in town?"

"Funny you should say ghost," he said as he passed a non-corporeal hand through the center of the great machine.

"No. You are not dead. This day has sucked enough, there is no way that you're gone too."

219

"Don't worry, it's cool." Said Matt. "I'm just extremely unconscious, this is my astral projection. Pretty cool, huh?"

Kiran sighed. "Super. Now get out of the way while I blow this sweet looking Kirby machine up before Cassie uses it to murder the crap out of us."

"You can't."

"Sure I can, it'll be fun. Watch me."

"Nope. Orders from el hefe Merlyn, we have to take a peek inside first."

"He's free?"

"Yup, just got him out of stir."

"Very cool. Then can we blow it up after?"

"You betcha."

"Awesome, so go make like Kitty Pryde and take a look."

"What? Oh right, yeah, forgot I could do that for a second. Back in a jiffy." With his body still half outside, Matt stuck his head into the machine, he looked like someone who'd lost his noggin to the guillotine.

"Gods, that's disturbing," said Kiran to his butt.

Matt yelled, "You have to get this thing opened right now!" Emerging from the machine his face was covered in terror. "Focus your fire on the edges and then pry it apart. She's in there!"

A torrent of concussive fire strikes hit the side of the machine, one after the other in small but controlled succession. Kiran kept hitting it until the front looked like a door hanging off of its hinges, she squeezed her fingers into the gap between the heated metal piece, without getting burned, and opened it to reveal the prisoner inside.

Gasping for fresh air, their lost friend, the real Cassie, fell to her knees. She was covered in dirt and grime, soaked in sweat, and dressed in ragged jeans and a faded Purple Rain tee; her hair had grown out since last they saw her, it hung to her shoulders, strawberry blonde with pink tips, the remnant of her last dye job before leaving on Summer vacation.

"Cassie!" Called Kiran and Matt.

"Oh my God." Said Matt.

"Are you okay?" Said Kiran. "Of course you're not, that's a really dumb question, I'm sorry. Stay here with Matt, I'll go get help."

Cassie grabbed Kiran's arm and held on tight, she looked at her, eyes full of madness and rage. "Where…is…she?"

"They're fighting her right now." Matt interrupted. "The wizard wanted me to bring you over there."

"What?" Said Kiran. "That's insane. You go float over there and tell Merlyn to forget it."

"No." Said Cassie. "I understand what I have to do. Take me to her, I owe that fucking witch the payback of a lifetime." She put her hand on the ground, trying to stand. "Kiran, help me up."

"Sure, just be careful, okay."

"Sorry, but I think we passed careful a hell of a long time ago." She stood, shaking. "I'm going to kill her."

"You might have to stand in line, she murdered Hannah's mom earlier today, girl's in full vengeance mode right now."

"Not Sarah," said Cassie. "We have to end this now, get me there quick. I'm afraid she already has enough juice to wipe us all out if we don't stop her in the next few minutes. We're still connected, I can feel the magicks inside of her taking hold, becoming greater."

"What was she doing with you?"

"She found me at the start of the summer, killed my mom, took my place, even killed dad before shutting me away in the machine beneath the city, her servants, they only brought me out long enough to keep my alive. Used me to siphon the chaos magic that she and the doctor stirred up from all of the killing and fear, by passing it through me into her she wasn't harmed by the raw energy."

"And you?"

"Don't know, I hope when all of this is over I'll be all right eventually."

"You will be." Said Kiran. "No way you're checking out after all of this."

"I'll certainly try my best."

The machine blew up in the background as Kiran tossed a giant fireball at it; the scene of the battle came into view as they stumbled down the park grounds, it was absolute anarchy. Merlyn and Allison fought one another in the sky, dueling like two forgotten gods vying for the attention of their mortal audience. Down below Hannah contended with the snake man, ducking streams of fire from his gullet and striking back with Doombringer, only to miss in return;

while the Monster of Frankenstein hacked and chopped his way through what was left of the witch's chemical warlocks.

"Stop for a second." Cassie stretched her arms high above her and closed her eyes. "I think I can take some of her power away from here," She said.

All of a sudden the super-witch, Allison stopped in midair; her eyes rolled back into her head, her skin grew pale, and she trembled as she started to fall. Merlyn looked below, saw what Cassie was doing and seized the opportunity, holding his scythe aloft he summoned a gale wind. The gust of air hit the witch like a kamikaze 747, throwing her straight through the front and back of the observatory's dome to the surface of the park where she landed, creating a giant crater.

Both Hannah and Colonel Hesse used the distraction to make short work of their foes; the colonel struck with precision and care, heaving his battleaxe through the air until the blade entered the top of one of the men's heads, cutting a hole down to his neck; turning from the fountain of gore pumping out of the poor bastard he blocked a binding spell from another warlock with his sword and pulled out his Desert Eagle, shooting him in the face, the resulting implosion/explosion left nothing but a bloody stump behind. Seeing his master driven from the sky threw the snake man into a rage, he charged at Hannah, with teeth bared and forked tongue exposed he set upon her, tried to overwhelm her with brute strength but was unsuccessful. She sliced him open across the middle, spilled his snakey guts on the ground, and flattened his head with the hammer.

As he twitched and bled out Hannah picked him up by the legs and tossed him into the gulley that rested at the bottom of the other side of the hill. For a moment she didn't move, and then realizing who was standing next to Kiran, she ran over to hug her friend. "You better be you this time."

"Yep, it's me!"

"Thank God, fake you was a real bitch."

"And that's being polite."

Amid the revelry Allison began to crawl out of the crater, sick and haggard, defeated, eyes hollow and dark, she gathered arcane black magic about her, muttered curses in forgotten languages and prepared to murder everyone, even at the cost of her own life. "Come here, girls. I WANT MY POWER BACK!"

Merlyn landed beside Cassie, put up a shield between them and the witch, then pushed it back, knocking her off balance. "I can only cut her off for a second, you both know what you have to do." Without hesitation, Hannah pulled the Dragon Blade from her belt and thrust it through the heart of Allison Kosh, her mother's lifelong best friend and killer, retrieving it as her implacable friend stepped up to the witch.

"That's the thing about being a conduit," said the real Cassie. "The magic flows both ways. It's time you felt what it's been like to be me these last couple of months. C'mere, you psycho bitch."

She snatched Allison by the the sides of her face, pressing her fingernails so hard that her tormentor's blood flowed from under them, they each screamed as tendrils of light erupted from Allison's eyes and mouth, affixing themselves in the same manner to Cassie. The immense magicks that the great machine had collected for months, siphoned and used for the darkest of purposes, all of it, every drop now flowed back into the frail form of a teenage girl with strawberry blonde pink hair who had been used to the point of physical and spiritual exhaustion. And she was fucking pissed.

The witch writhed in agony as the real Cassie stole her power, her paper thin skin tore throughout her body, blood trickled down her limbs and inch by terrible inch she died an excruciating death. The tendrils faded and Cassie pushed her away; Allison Kosh, the Witch of Wichita, the most talented witch-breed of her generation, hit the ground like a sack of unwanted garbage. Black smoke drifted from her withered husk, wind tore the dried flesh from her body, until all that was left were her yellowed bones lying in the dirt.

"ANNIHILARE!" A giant fireball reduced the bones to ash, and left the deep crater to smoke behind her, Cassie beamed with satisfaction as she walked away.

"Well done." Said Merlyn. He walked up next to her, laid his right hand on her heart and whispered an inaudible spell. "There, that should help with the pain."

"Thank you," she said. Without warning Hannah and Kiran snatched up Cassie and smothered her with two giant hugs, the three girls laughed until they ran out of breath. "Okay okay, guys, I love you too but you're gonna squeeze the pee out of me if you don't let go."

"I knew you weren't evil!" Yelled Kiran as she jumped up and down.

"Was there ever a doubt?" Said Cassie.

"Nah," said Hannah. "We knew it the whole time."

"Yeah right. To be fair though, she did make a pretty convincing me. That was part of the connection, she didn't just look like me, she really became me in a lot of ways."

"But just a little eviler," said Kiran.

"Oh, way way, eviler," said Hannah. "Better hair too."

"Shush you." Said Cassie. They all burst out laughing again,

"Hey guys," said Ghost Matt, he was standing just to the side and he was flickering there and not there like a spectral lamp. "I think Zeke's found me, I can kinda hear him."

Merlyn ceased talking to Colonel Hesse. "You need to get back to your body right now," he said. "It's important you wake up so they can help you, if not, your physical form may expire."

"Um, how do I do that?"

"I will guide you—simply let go. Projecting your astral self takes effort, your natural state is to be with your body. You should be able to snap back. Instead of focusing on here, on being present, let your consciousness drift away, like a fallen tree branch caught in a river current."

"Okay, man. Let's give it a go."

The wizard pursed his lips and blew at the not quite ghost until it turned into a whistle. Matt saw himself fade away, felt his body lift into the air, it was slow at first, then sudden and jarring as he rushed over Serenity and crashed back into his own body. Gasping for air he shot upright, saw Zeke and an EMT hovering, and noticed that he was in an ambulance. Overwhelming pain shot through him, a burning discomfort, *oh Christ,* he thought, *I'm being burned alive.* The EMT shoved a needle into his arm, full of something soothing, Matt let out a relieved breath and closed his eyes.

"Well?" Demanded Kiran.

"He's fine," said Merlyn. "Back in his own body and being taken care of. I sensed that he has a concussion and a bunch of broken bones but nothing he won't recover from."

Hannah took his arm and touched his cheek. "Thank you," she said.

"You're welcome."

"Y'know, for a badass wizard you blush pretty easily, Mr. Merlyn Morningstar." She ran her fingers along the black twisted horns protruding out from under his hairline, the serrated ridges climbing like rungs on a ladder from base to pointy end on both of them. With her hand on the back of his neck she pulled him closer and kissed him, long and soul quenching, like a couple dying of thirst finally taking a drink of water.

"What do you think?" Said Merlyn pointing to the horns.

"I like 'em, makes you look all wicked badass and stuff." She smiled widely at him, relieved and happy for a change, a respite amid all of the horror and loss. "Besides, I like a little monster in my man."

227

"Might be more than a little, I had to make a literal deal with the devil."

"Your dad, right?"

"Uh huh, how'd you know?

"I'm good at filling in the blanks from vague conversations." She paused. "Don't worry about it, you'll beat him. You're Merlyn Morningstar, Chronomancer, Battlemage; the only person the devil fears, is you. Never forget that."

"My Huntress." Merlyn embraced her again and leaned her back, doing his best to reenact the famous sailor and nurse VJ Day kiss.

Hannah busted up laughing. "Silly sweet wizard." She said as she bumped him in the chest with her fist and pecked him on the cheek. Hand in hand they stared into each other's eyes and just smiled, trying their best to make the moment stretch as far as possible.

The celebration was halted by a series of sudden weirdness; Frankenstein's Monster leaped out of the way of a deep chasm that ripped through the courtyard, a flock of birds dropped dead out of the sky, pipes from beneath the surface began to erupt sending the water flowing upwards, fallen zombies began to sing in inhuman voices, trees shed their leaves and wilted until they were petrified, animals and insects departed the area in noticeable number; and as the world turned upside down Cassie screamed as she leveled the observatory apartments with a neon green blast of mystical plasma that could be seen from three counties away.

"Damn it," said Merlyn as he ran to Cassie's side. "She's absorbed too much of the chaos magic into herself."

"What does that mean?" Asked Hannah.

"Imagine pouring the raging ocean into a water glass, she can't contain all of that power, in a few minutes she's going to undergo the equivalent of a supernatural Chernobyl."

"She's going to die?"

"And take the entire Midwest with her."

"Did you know this might happen?" Asked Kiran.

Merlyn stopped and considered what to say next. "Yes. I thought this could be the result of her taking the witch's power away. Allison was a trained practitioner with decades of experience and immense natural ability, Cassie had the beginnings of talent, but she's new to it and can't handle the forces within her." He knelt next to Cassie and whispered a couple of spells, attempting to calm her suffering. "I hoped that this wouldn't be the case, but magic has its own rules and its own consequences."

Flames surrounded Kiran as she seized an orb of fire in her left hand, ready to be thrown. "You knew!" She screamed. "You knew this would happen and you didn't warn her. YOU BASTARD!"

Merlyn snapped his fingers. Kiran's flames immediately ceased. "That's my wizard blood that courses through your veins, remember? Don't think for a second that you can use my own power against me."

"Enough!" Snapped Hannah. "There isn't time for this. What can we do?"

"Nothing," said Merlyn. "I have to take her away from here. I'll travel forward to a time and place where she won't be able to harm anyone."

"You're someone that can be harmed!" Exclaimed Hannah.

"I'll be weak but I can use the explosion to ride a temporal wave out of there."

"Will you come back?"

"I don't know, it'll be a blind jump, I could end up almost anywhere at anytime."

"Well once you end up anywhere and anytime, you come right back here. Okay?"

"Sounds like a great plan to me." He kissed her lightly on the lips and she embraced him, not letting go. "I will come back, I promise."

Hannah released him, hesitant but resigned to what had to be done. "You better, wizard boy."

Cassie was delirious, unresponsive to her friends' attempts to talk to her, yelling and thrashing about in pain. Merlyn picked her up and walked as far away from everyone as he could, then laid her down next to the tall observatory building that housed the telescope. He raised his reaper's scythe and spoke the incantation, **"KRONOS QUAESO ERIPIAS ME!"** The ground and the buildings shook as a tempest of swirling shapes and sounds appeared around the two of them. "Remember," he shouted across the courtyard to Hannah. "You can be whoever you want to be. Don't let the future change who you are. I'm sorry I can't stay, I lov…"

A flash of white light consumed Merlyn and Cassie, the wind howled and echoed off of the surrounding hills as the temporal storm cascaded out, threatening to overtake everyone as they ran for their lives from the explosion.

Minutes later the group stopped running as they reached the bottom of the hill near the school. Hannah looked up, there was nothing left, the whole observatory, buildings and the part of the hill they had stood on were no more, only a smoking crater and a hillside on fire remained. While Kiran and Colonel Hesse dusted themselves off she walked over and sat beneath a big oak tree, stared up at the spot where the observatory should have been and let herself cry, but only for a minute. Then she noticed how the leaves were blowing in the wind, the world had survived, wiping her tears away she began to smile. "I love you too." Hannah said aloud.

Chapter 14: Twisted

Six hours later Samuel sat in a hidden hollow at the bottom of the hill, beaten, broken, breathing heavy, and sweating from exhaustion; moving carefully he extended his left leg, twisting and snapping the bones until they fell into their proper place, the skin elongated to conform to the new shape of his leg and as he stood his foot popped and reset itself as he stepped on to the ground. He stretched his arms out, straightened his back and stood up tall. No need to hide, not anymore, his long role as Shelley's Igor was now concluded. A thousand of years of planning and plotting and now the pieces were almost in place. *Victor Frankenstein had been a fool,* he thought, *but a useful one, the witch, she had been easier to manipulate than I would have ever believed possible. So much history, so much put in motion, and nobody has ever known my true name... soon that will change.*

Samuel climbed to the top of the hill, the smoke from the dying fire that had consumed the observatory rose into the night's sky, the full moon above painted red from the reflection of the supernatural blaze. The ruins of the observatory lay all around the hillside; still smoldering from the final flickering of the supernatural flames, they had seared the landscape with an unholy heat, patches of glass formed where the fire had touched the sand and the soil. Stillness surrounded the hilltop, nothing moved or made a sound; neither man or beast, nor tree or shrub, there was no wind and even the fire itself was dying out at last.

Standing as still as a statue he waited there patiently until the break of dawn when he saw a woman walk up the path from the school to the ruined observatory. Her dark hair framed her ageless marble face as it glowed in the light of the early morning; she wore a blood splattered Sex Pistols t-shirt over a long sleeveless black dress cinched with a brown belt, sandals of a likewise earthen hue, a broad silver choker with a cross worked into the center, and in her right hand she carried her mother's warhammer.

As she approached him she smiled widely showing her fangs and said, "Well done, my friend."

"Thank you."

"And is your partner pleased?"

"Very much so," said Samuel. "Your plans coincide with ours, my lady. This alliance is beneficial to all of us."

"Mmm…yes," she said. "And with my plan you didn't die at the end, dear sir. Do not forget that."

"As you say," said Samuel with a bow. "What are your thoughts on the outcome?"

"The wizard was almost too easy to fool; an outfit change, some pre-planned sound effects and pyrotechnics was all it took to convince him that I was her. I'm just lucky he didn't notice the different t-shirt you brought me earlier." Vannah paused, and surveyed the destruction. "Everything happened exactly as I remembered it, except for your death of course, and what follows next. It's unfortunate that I couldn't thank your sorceress friend for this idea; I played my part to perfection, far better than she did, but I suppose killing Allison twice for murdering my mother will have to do. It's funny, even now a part of me wishes that I could have saved her. How myopic and human of me."

"What of the girl? Did you kill her?"

"Trapped in the castle on the other side. I couldn't risk her demise without knowing what it would do to me."

"Sensible precaution, unless she escapes of course."

"Don't worry about that, I fully expect her to escape, after all, I did. By that point however the timelines will have diverged enough that killing her will no longer be a problem."

"Of course. And what of the boy with the connection to the Witchery Way?"

"In the hospital, the other one found him," she said. "He's perfect for our long term plans."

"Excellent, shall I begin?" Asked Samuel.

"Yes," she replied. "It's finally time to bring back The Servants of Darkness. The new future begins now." Vannah threw her head back and laughed, the picture of a villain from some forgotten Saturday serial matinee. The man beside her began to change, muscles snapped, bones broke, and skin stretched until the ancient snake man took his place. Inclining her head she stepped back as the ophidian raised his arms and spoke in the dead demonic language of the Atlantean serpent people, guttural words rang out across the landscape that had not been said on Earth in tens of thousands of years, prayers to long abandoned gods echoed into the night, lightning and thunder crashed above them.

Vannah seized the warhammer in both hands, ran screaming towards the ruins of the observatory and swung with all of her considerable strength at nothing whatsoever, and as she backed away the sky before her tore itself open. It appeared as a crack at first, as if a bolt of lightning had become stuck in midair five feet atop of the ground, and then it widened, a couple of inches and then more until it was the size of a door. And beyond that door was hell, the shadows and the fires through the portal swirled and pushed against each other for dominance; the landscape was barren, rotten, and constantly aflame. A cold blue sun hung in the atmosphere illuminating the sulfurous haze that stretched over the land and the gray nebulous clouds that drifted overhead.

"Ssspeak their namesss," hissed the ophidian. "Call them back to thisss world."

Vannah spread her arms wide and gazed into the doorway to hell, she shouted, "William, The Cursed, I call thee!" The ground began to shake as she continued to speak. "Zhu Jiangshi, Son of the Dragon, I call thee! Igazi Idemoni, I call thee!" Storm clouds gathered above, the wind howled, lightning split the sky, thunder boomed in the distance, and rain soaked the land. "Senyaka, The Nightsister, I call thee!" A rolling wall of fog spread across the hills and the valleys to the city below . "Catherine Lestrange, I call thee!" And above the blood moon blotted out the rising sun covering the countryside in a supernatural nightfall. "I even saved the best for last," said Vannah with a chilling laugh. "Vlad Tepes, The Impaler, Pui de Drac, Dracul,

Saul Bishop

MOTHERFUCKING DRACULA, KING OF THE VAMPIRES, I CALL THEE!

Vampires started to emerge from the gateway, emaciated creatures, wretches more resembling victims of concentration camps and famine than of powerful beings of myth and legend. Two of them came staggering and shaking out of the portal side be side, a man and a woman wearing rags, leaning against the other, holding each other up. At once they were joined by another and then another, two more women, naked and skeletal. Vannah beckoned them to come closer, they all circled, surrounding her like a pack of staving dogs.

The male advanced towards her, low to the ground, his head cocked sideways, "Hungry," wheezed the vampire.

"It'll be okay, sweetums," said Vannah as she put her fingers under his chin and delicately kissed him on his parchment thin lips. "I called for take out. Should be here any minute, just in time for the rest of your friends to join us."

Moments passed and one more appeared out of the gate, dressed in tattered and filthy once colorful silks with gaudy long fingernails adorned in fine jewels, Zhu Jiangshi, Son of the Dragon. This vampire did not circle or succumb to an animal nature, he merely looked at the sky and then inclined his head in a gesture of respect to his rescuers.

Bowing to the elder vampire, Vannah said, "You honor me with your courtesy and patience, Master Zhu. I can

236

scarcely begin to understand the depths of your hunger, a meal will soon arrive."

The last of the six servants of darkness came forth from the hellish aperture looking as if he had recently left a dinner party, aside from the dirt and mud covering his gray suit his appearance was splendid and he conveyed all of the aspects of a healthy man in his early forties, albeit in need of a shave and a bath. His hair was black with shocks of white around the temples, untidy but not too long, and his beard was far more Miami Vice than hipster chic. It was remarkable but Dracula looked way more like an older Cary Grant than he did Bela Lugosi or even Christopher Lee.

"Welcome home, Lord Dracul." Said Vannah.

The King of the Vampires confronted her, he closed his eyes, smelled the air, and with a surprising sudden flash he grabbed her arm, pulling her against him he touched her cheek, then whispered in her ear, "How curious that the daughter of my jailers would be my savior. You have my gratitude, my dear." As he released her he turned his back to view the city below. "Ah, the North American Convergence. Now tell me, hybrid, why have you released me and my kind from our torment?"

"In due time, my lord," said Vannah. "I believe that breakfast has arrived." Headlights peered through the fog as a car wound its way up the road to the top of the hill and the ruined observatory. It was an old green Land Rover, there was a middle age man driving along with an attractive woman near the same age in the passenger seat, riding in the back was their little boy, it was the doctor and his family that Hannah had saved from the mugger the night before. Their vehicle came to a stop with the lights still on about fifty yards from Vannah and her new friends, she softened her features to appear more human and went over to them, as she came into sight she waved and smiled, everyone in the car did the same, in particular the boy who was beaming with excitement. The doctor rolled down the driver's side window as she stood next to him, "Oh, thank God you're here. I wasn't sure you would come when I called," she said.

"Of course we came," said Doctor Winslow. "Even Tommy wouldn't let us leave the house without him. He says we owe you, and we certainly do. You sounded urgent on the phone, how can I help?"

She heard the vampires near silent advance as they flanked both sides of the vehicle, taking several steps back she said, "You already have." The creatures struck at the father first, tearing the car door off its hinges and dragging him shouting to the ground fifteen yards away, the male and the female that had come through the portal together tore him apart in a frenzy of feeding. As the mother began to scream her window burst open and she was hauled kicking and punching out of the vehicle by a torrent of dirty clawed hands, the other three feasted on her without tearing her apart but by sinking their teeth deep into her arteries. Moments passed as pain turned to pleasure and she died moaning in rapturous delight. The little boy sobbed and yelled in panic while he watched his parents being murdered by monsters; Vannah opened the back door, was gentle picking him up and said in a soft voice, "Shhh, shhh, shhh, It's going to be all right, Tommy. I'll take care of you."

"Please, Hannah, please," pleaded Tommy through his sniffling and gasping for air. "You have to save them, you have to save my mom and dad."

"Don't you worry, we're going to fix everything." She carried the little boy over to Dracula, set him on the ground, held his hand and presented him to the vampire. "For you, my lord."

"Mmm…innocence," said Dracula. "But will he be enough? It has been two decades since I've fed."

"He will be more than enough, not only will you consume him now but you will consume all that he will every be. In my future this one is a legendary hero that battles the darkness, he is loved by millions. Take him and that bright tomorrow of possibilities ends now."

"My dear, you are just full of surprises." Vannah let go of his shaking hand as Dracula said, "Come here, boy."

Tommy walked towards Dracula and then looked back at Vannah. "You're not a hero," he said. "You're a monster."

"I know," she replied.

The King of the Vampires lowered himself onto one knee to speak to the boy. "Do not be frightened, child," he said. "It is a blessing to be released from this tiresome existence." In an instant he opened the child's throat with his razor sharp fingernails and began to feed. Tommy didn't cry, he didn't wail, he had no time to speak, he simply died, and all of his tomorrows and all of the people he would have saved ceased to be along with him.

Dracula let the dead boy drop to the dirt as he rose, he looked like a man in the prime of his life, the gauntness was gone, he no longer looked exhausted and his face had a pink glow after having fed.

"Feeling better?" Asked Vannah.

"Much. My compliments on your preparation this evening." The other vampires returned as he finished speaking, the before and after difference was astounding, where minutes ago they had been skeletons with skin, now the other five were the pinnacle of physical fitness. Albeit covered in blood and sweat and dirt, clothed in rags or else naked, still they all basked in the marvel that they had been set free from hell. "My friends," said Dracula. "How very wonderful it is to see you all healthy again."

One of the Vampires approached Vannah and sneered. "I cannot believe that I have a mongrel hybrid to thank for my freedom." William the Cursed was a handsome man, he spoke with a highborn British accent and even covered with dirt and grime his blonde hair shined like an Angel's. Vannah cut off his head in one swing with the half-moon axe side of her warhammer, she smashed his skull to bits once it hit the ground and watched as the torso began to combust, burning to ash and bone.

"Sorry about that," said Vannah. "Any other complaints?"

A beautiful woman with a slender body and silver hair spoke up, her face was ageless and angular, her skin looked like cream flush with pink highlights after having eaten and she had a rich French cadence to her English speech, it was the vampire that had accompanied William through the portal. Catherine Lestrange said, "My dear, you have saved me twice, first from an eternity in hell and then from an eternity with that fool who attached himself to me. I am in your debt."

"Nice to hear," said Vannah as she leaned on the bloody warhammer resting against the ground. "You can repay me with a seat at your little Dark Illuminati table, looks like you have an opening."

"No hybrid has ever been one of the six!" Shouted Zhu Jiangshi.

"Until now," said Vannah. "It's a new millennium, Master Zhu, as well as the year of the monkey, change is the only constant the world knows anymore."

"I have no problem with this," said Catherine Lestrange. "Another woman in our ranks pleases me, perhaps she will teach us all great things."

"What say you, Senyaka the Nightsister and Igazi Idemoni?" Asked Dracula.

Igazi merely bowed her head to a slight degree in acquiescence, whereas Senyaka stared at Vannah for a full minute before she said, "Yes."

Dracula put his hand on Jiangshi's shoulder and said to him, "I'm sorry, old friend, but I must concur, she has saved us from imprisonment and eliminated one of the six. To join us is her right. For now." He sliced his right palm with his fingernail and went over to her, extending his hand, Vannah did the same and grasped his hand, the surge of power she felt was intoxicating. She repeated the process four more times with the others, each mingling of the blood leaving her further delighted and tipsy with mystical dynamism. "Welcome to the Six Servants of Darkness, child."

As Vannah reveled in the new power surging throughout her body the snake-man joined their discussion, standing behind Vannah with crossed arms his presence loomed above the others. An eight foot tall monster from mythology and time immemorial, the group had paid little attention to him until now, but all of that changed as they looked at him up close, even Dracula seemed to be impressed by the creature. He pointed towards the aperture to Duat that remained open a few yards from them. "It isss time," Samuel hissed.

"I'd ask where he came from," said Dracula. "But I imagine the answer is a lengthy one for another time."

"Smart Count," said Vannah. "And Samuel is correct, it is time."

"For what?" Asked Catherine.

"To call all of your friends home, of course." Said Vannah. "You didn't think that I pulled all of this off just for you, did you?" Singing *You're So Vain* in a loud obnoxious voice she walked over to the side of the hill to peer down at the city. "I did all of this and more to turn that city, the holy fucking convergence into an abattoir of fear and death! Now turn on your evil bat-signal or whatever and get them the hell out of hell already."

"You are rude and impudent, and in any other century I'd be baying for your blood, but for now I concur." The King of the Vampires walked over to the open gateway and closed his eyes while he touched his temples with the tips of his fingers.

"Welcome to Professor V's School for Gifted Vampires," said Vannah. "Even I can feel the psychic pull."

"It is done," said Dracula as he walked away from the portal.

"How long and how many?" Asked Vannah.

"Not long," he answered. "Our prison dimension was surprisingly finite, like a map with edges and endings, most of us didn't wander far. As for how many, I'm not sure, your mother banished every vampire on Earth no matter where they were at the time."

"Knock it off," she said. "You're the king vamp and you're psychic, make an educated guess."

"Ten thousand," he said. "Unlike humans we have never wanted our population to get out of control."

"Smart," said Vannah. "Why create too much unneeded competition over your food supply."

"Precisely, by our very nature we are superior to the humans in every way, we don't kill each other unless it becomes necessary, and there is always plenty to eat in this world."

The hill began to shake and the gateway widened, tearing crossways as the vampires started to come through en masse, they were pathetic creatures; as starved, emaciated, filthy and feral as her new companions had been at first. Dracula psychically directed them towards the city and as they came through the gate they turned and ran down the hillside to the unsuspecting populace below.

The horde of starving vampires descended onto Serenity, and twenty years of hunger and rage went with them, they shrieked and they wailed, they tore at each other, they ripped apart everything in their path. Like a biblical flood or a cleansing fire they fell upon the city and spread out to every street and home in front of them. Within minutes of their arrival the screams of their first victims reached the top of the hill, painful cries full of misery and sudden terror that grew louder and louder, a cacophony of suffering that resounded throughout the entire countryside.

"Well isn't that a marvelous sight," said Vannah. The wind blew her black hair about and she laughed, delighting in the destruction; obstacles had been removed, her enemies were defeated and now it was time to advance her plans. As the vampire smiled she recalled something she'd said to her younger self on the other side, *That son of a bitch doesn't want to stop the apocalypse, he wants to win it.* She considered that for a moment as she watched and listened to the carnage below, *And so do I.*

Epilogue: Egypt 1925

The voyage home from India to Egypt had been a difficult one, weeks spent at sea and more travelling over land, delirious with fever, replete with visions. But now he was home. "I have to write it all down, to warn her what's coming." Elias Kord sat at his desk overlooking Cairo, the Great Pyramids in the distance, Art Deco buildings dotting the landscape, mud brick houses filling in the spaces between, and the colorful markets with their vendors shouting to be heard; he wrote at a furious pace, covering page after page in tiny scrawl with details of what he'd seen and what he still remembered. The images were fading fast from his mind.

Desert sand and a warm breeze blew through the open windows on the sides of the room, stirring the stagnant hot air in his second story apartment; papers, stacked high, fell from their perches, floating around the room, settling beneath couches and in far corners, Elias had long since abandoned trying to keep order when working. Lost in thought and distant prophecy he was startled as a giant mummy burst through the door, shredding the solid cherry wood like papyrus, crossed the floor, picked him up, and slammed him into the wall face first.

Muezzins atop their towers called for midday prayer as Hannah crashed through the great circular glass window adorning Kord's home, the curved blade of her khopesh gleaming in the afternoon sun as she swung it at the desiccated walking corpse. She took his arms off, freeing Elias, and with her next blow, severed his head, watching as it rolled to the foot of a nearby couch piled high with books and artifacts. The mummy's body hit the floor, making a loud thud and sending a cloud of dust into the room, choking the air. Hannah sheathed her sword in the leather scabbard she wore on her right side, buttoning the concaved metal in so that it was secure.

A glowing red light shined from the recess of where Hannah's left eye should have been and her same arm whirred and hissed as the cogs and gears beneath the iron surface worked to keep the artificial appendage moving. Her white hair was accented with streaks of silver and fixed in a loose bun with jade chopsticks through it; she wore an ivory button down shirt, the sleeves rolled up, khaki slacks, and brown boots. Over her shoulder was a leather knapsack containing rolled up pieces of parchment sticking out of the top. She threw the bag on the chair by the desk, unrolled one of the papers inside and set it down, revealing a map of Northern Africa covered in hieroglyphics and a half dozen other forgotten arcane languages.

"Elias Kord, my name is Hannah Harrison, I need your help returning to the future."

To Be Continued In...

Hannah The Huntress - Book 2: The Servants of Darkness

Winter 2017

Things To Come...

- The Return
- "Hi, I'm Melvin, the Wolf-Man."
- Frankenstein's Monster Vs. Dracula
- The Assassins of Anubis and the Black Pyramid
- "I've always been in love with you, I was just too afraid to say anything."
- The End

www.ingramcontent.com/pod-product-compliance
Lightning Source LLC
Chambersburg PA
CBHW051943220626
47052CB00004B/768